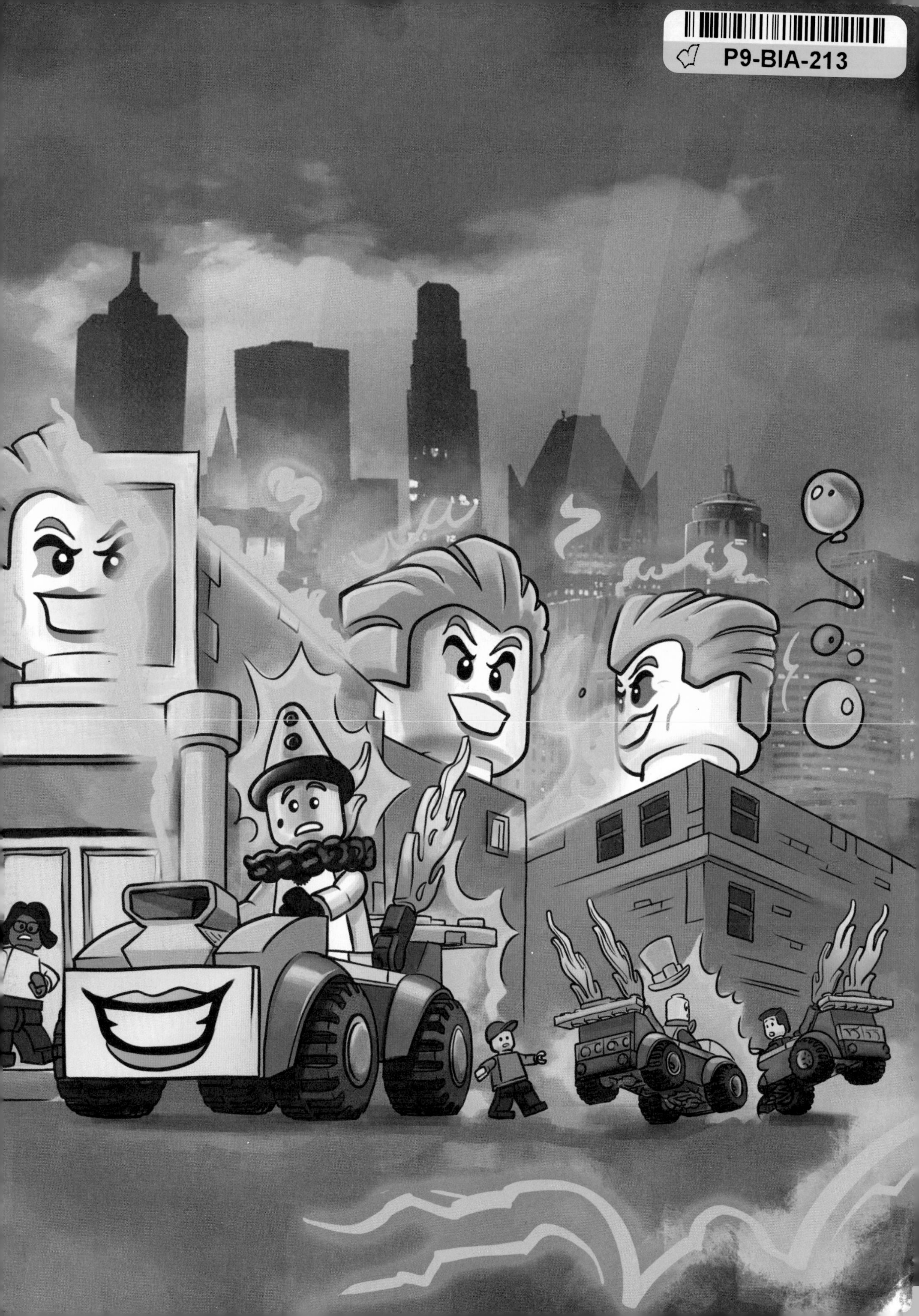

LEGO

BATMAN'S
5-MINUTE STORIES

LEGO BATMAN

BATMAN'S
5-MINUTE
STORIES

Random House 🏠 New York

Illustrated by
AMEET Studio

Published in the United States by Random House Children's Books, a division of Penguin Random House LLC, 1745 Broadway, New York, NY 10019, and in Canada by Penguin Random House Canada Limited, Toronto. Random House and the colophon are registered trademarks of Penguin Random House LLC.

rhcbooks.com

Educators and librarians, for a variety of teaching tools, visit us at RHTeachersLibrarians.com

ISBN 978-0-593-38136-6 (trade) — ISBN 978-0-593-38137-3 (ebook)

MANUFACTURED IN CHINA

10 9 8 7 6 5 4 3 2 1

Random House Children's Books supports the First Amendment and celebrates the right to read.

CONTENTS

THE ZOO TAKEOVER

Based on the story by Liz Marsham

It is a big day in Gotham City—the zoo is about to reopen! Billionaire Bruce Wayne and the mayor are there for the celebration—but then the animals all escape! Something that wild may be more than Batman can handle on his own. The Caped Crusader calls in his allies to save the day—and to find out who is behind this dangerous disorder.

"Gotham City Zoo is ready to reopen!" the mayor announced happily. And now, thanks to a generous donation from billionaire Bruce Wayne—the animals will have new, high-tech homes."

But then . . . *rrrrrrrrrumble.*

"Do you hear that?" the mayor asked Bruce. *Rrrrrrrrrrummmmmmmble!*

"It sounds like—" Bruce began.

CREAK. Suddenly, the zoo gates began to swing open on their own.

"No, it's not a *creak*," said the mayor. "It's more like a—"

RRRRUMMMMBBBBLE!

"Mayor, look out!" shouted Bruce, pulling her aside just in time.

With a crash, the gates broke open, and a stampede of animals burst through! Elephants, giraffes, gorillas, and cheetahs stormed the gates as the crowd ran in all directions. Finally, a colony of penguins came waddling out of the zoo, squawking with alarm.

"Call Commissioner Gordon!" the mayor told Bruce, getting to her feet.

As soon as the mayor turned away, he tapped on his ear to activate his hidden communicator.

"Alfred," he barked. "Are you—"

"Yes, Master Bruce," came Alfred's voice. "It's all over the news. Shall I alert the authorities?"

"Yes. And, Alfred," said Bruce, "call for backup."

Bruce ran back to join the mayor.

"How did this happen?" she asked. "Did something go wrong with the doors?"

"No," said Bruce firmly. "Someone did this on purpose. The question is why."

Moments later, Bruce Wayne put on his suit and became Batman! As he clicked his Utility Belt into place, the other Super Heroes arrived to help. Batman quickly gave The Flash, Supergirl, Green Lantern, and Aquaman their orders. They split up through the city to find the animals.

The Flash raced the cheetahs back to the zoo one by one, holding out bags of kitty treats to encourage them to follow him.

Green Lantern found the giraffes grazing in the park. He used his power ring to form a long set of harnesses around their heads and necks and gently guided them home.

"Two, four, six, eight! Get these apes back through the gates!" cheered Supergirl.

"Excellent job, everyone," said Batman. He and Batgirl rode two of the elephants back into the zoo. Then he saw Aquaman standing idly by the gift shop. "Aquaman, status report."

"Well, Batman," Aquaman said, strolling over, "those penguins know the King of Atlantis when they see him . . . I mean me! I just looked in their direction and they went straight back to their habitat. I didn't even have to use my sea creature telepathy!"

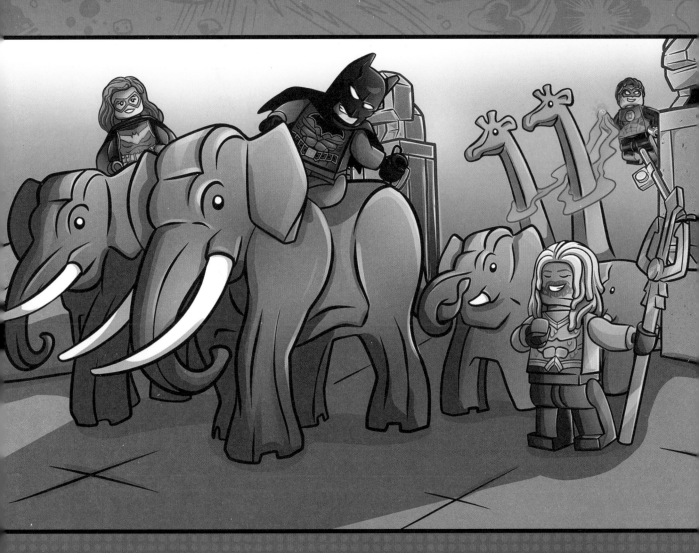

"The penguins went back on their own? Hmm . . ." Batman thought about that for a moment.

"What are you thinking, Batman?" Batgirl asked.

"Nothing yet," replied Batman. "What's important is that all the animals are safe. Good work, Justice League."

"Any time, Caped Crusader!" Green Lantern said.

"Thanks for the invite to your fancy zoo!" said Supergirl, flying off toward Metropolis.

Back in the Batcave, Batman watched the night's news on the Batcomputer, and his eyes went wide.

"Alfred, look at this!" Batman said. "While we were rounding up escaped animals, someone stole several necklaces from jewelry stores near the zoo!"

The butler shook his head sadly.

"But why take only the necklaces?"

"Perhaps, Master Bruce, the thieves had necks but no hands!" Alfred joked.

"That's it, Alfred!" Batman cried.

Batman quickly activated his Justice League communicator. "Aquaman, are you there?"

"Sea King here!" Aquaman replied. "What can I do for you?"

"Aquaman, when the penguins were heading back to the zoo, did you notice anything strange about them?"

"Well . . . ," Aquaman said after a pause, "now that you mention it, some of their necklaces were on backward."

"The penguins were wearing necklaces, and you didn't think to mention that?" growled Batman.

Batman leapt up from his chair. "There's only one person who could be behind this: Oswald Cobblepot—better known as The Penguin! I have to get back to the zoo right away!"

Stepping in front of him, Alfred said, "Sir, if Mr. Cobblepot is somehow controlling dozens of penguins, who knows what else he's up to?"

Batman jumped into the Batmobile. "There's no time. The Penguin could get away!" He revved the engine, and with the screech of tires, raced off toward the Gotham City Zoo!

Outside the penguin habitat, Batman paused, then took the side door that led to the underwater gallery. He could hear The Penguin cackling to himself, but he couldn't see the villain or his penguin army.

What he could see, directly across from him, was a large steel machine. It had several dish antennas and was emitting a strange humming noise.

"The penguins are being controlled by a machine beneath the penguin habitat," Batman said into his communicator.

Suddenly, all the lights came on. It was The Penguin, pointing one of his special umbrellas right at Batman! The umbrella's tip pulsed with light. Batman glanced back at the mind-control machine—the lights on the umbrella and the machine matched.

Cobblepot must be using this umbrella to give the penguins commands! he deduced.

Just as Batman finished that thought, a wave of penguins pushed forward and surrounded him. The Penguin motioned with his umbrella, and Batman was lifted and carried up the stairs to the main penguin habitat.

There, Batman saw even more stolen necklaces in a pile among the penguins.

"Now, where was I?" he mused. "Ah, yes, the diamonds." As he stuffed the necklaces into a bag, he said over his shoulder, "See, Batman, when we fight one-on-one, I always lose. But this time, you didn't expect me to have so many friends, did you?"

Batman smiled. "Oh, but I did," he replied.

The Penguin straightened in surprise.

Behind The Penguin, a green glow snagged his umbrella. "I'll hold that for you," said Green Lantern.

At the same time, several Batarangs hit the mind-control machine, smashing it into pieces.

"One mind-control machine on the fritz!" announced Batgirl.

"*WAUGH!*" cried Cobblepot. "Penguins, attack!" But the penguins didn't do anything.

"I don't think you speak their language anymore," said Aquaman.

"You see, Cobblepot," said Batman, "I wanted you to catch me. It gave my friends time to sneak in here. And now we can't wait to visit the new penguin exhibit . . . in Arkham Asylum!"

FREEZING COLD!

Based on the story by **Liz Marsham**

Mr. Freeze and Captain Cold have teamed up! The icy crooks want to make it winter in Gotham City—in the middle of summer! But Batman knows it takes a team of Super Heroes to beat a team of Super-Villains. He calls his friends Superman and Supergirl to help give the villains a warm welcome! When the battle heats up, will the Super Heroes be able to keep their cool?

The calendar said August, but in Gotham City, it looked and felt more like January! Icicles hung from trees, snow drifted down to pile up in the streets, and the air got colder and colder. A few hours ago, it had been just another hot and humid day. What was going on?

Batman drove through the chilly city in the Batmobile, staring at the snow and ice. "Alfred," he said into his earpiece, "I don't like this."

"Nor do I, Master Bruce," replied Alfred.

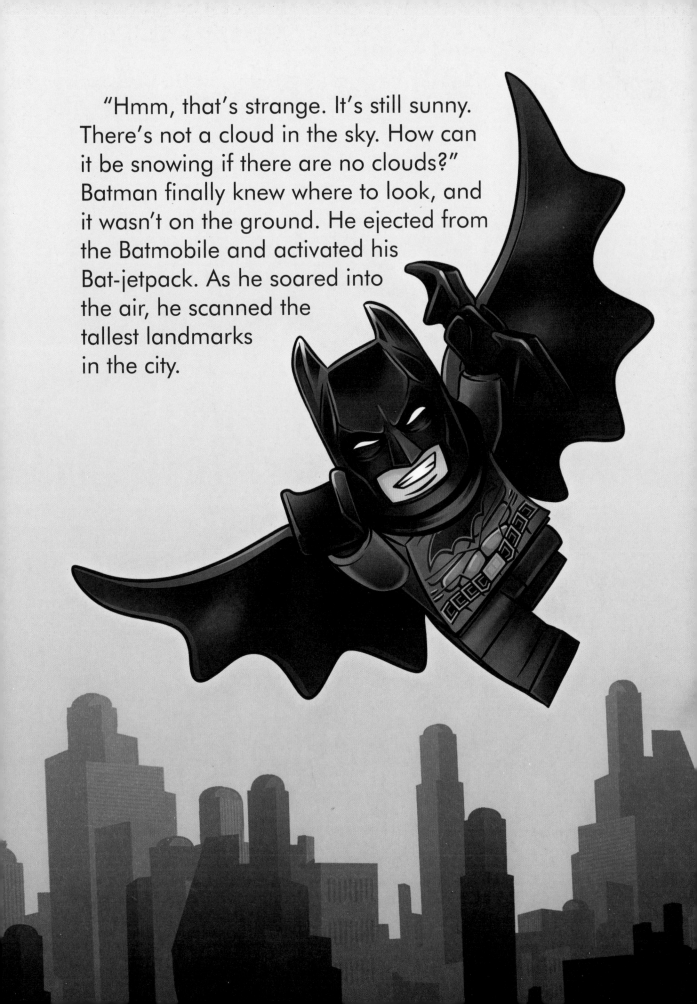

"Hmm, that's strange. It's still sunny. There's not a cloud in the sky. How can it be snowing if there are no clouds?" Batman finally knew where to look, and it wasn't on the ground. He ejected from the Batmobile and activated his Bat-jetpack. As he soared into the air, he scanned the tallest landmarks in the city.

"Why are there satellite dishes at the top of Wayne Tower?" Batman asked himself. "I didn't sign off on any new construction."

The shiny dishes sparkled and twinkled in the sun. Something about the way they caught the light was strange. As he got closer, it began to make sense: the dishes were made of glass, which was why they sparkled. And the twinkles were snow and ice crystals, shooting from the dishes and falling onto the city!

"Alfred, these aren't satellite dishes," Batman reported. "They look like Captain Cold's gun, only much bigger."

As Batman swung around the corner of the tower, he got a clear look behind the dishes. "This machinery is much too complex for Captain Cold to set up on his own. In fact, these hoses and wires look like the work of . . ."

Just then, a figure stepped out. It was a man dressed in a bulky metallic suit with a glass helmet. He pointed a freeze ray with a large nozzle on the end at Batman. It was Mr. Freeze!

He fired a ray at Batman. A beam of blue energy shot out toward the Dark Knight, who barely dodged it.

"Mr. Freeze!" Batman responded, swooping back to hover in front of the villain. "I knew you had to be involved in this. Give up now!"

"Ah, but, Batman," chuckled Mr. Freeze, "you forget. I'm not alone!"

Batman gasped as a freezing-cold blast hit him in the side. Captain Cold had been hiding just out of sight! Batman's jetpack sputtered and died as the cold blast hit it, and a moment later, Batman's torso was entirely encased in ice.

Batman had only a few seconds. "Alfred!" he shouted into his communicator.

"Already done, sir," Alfred replied.

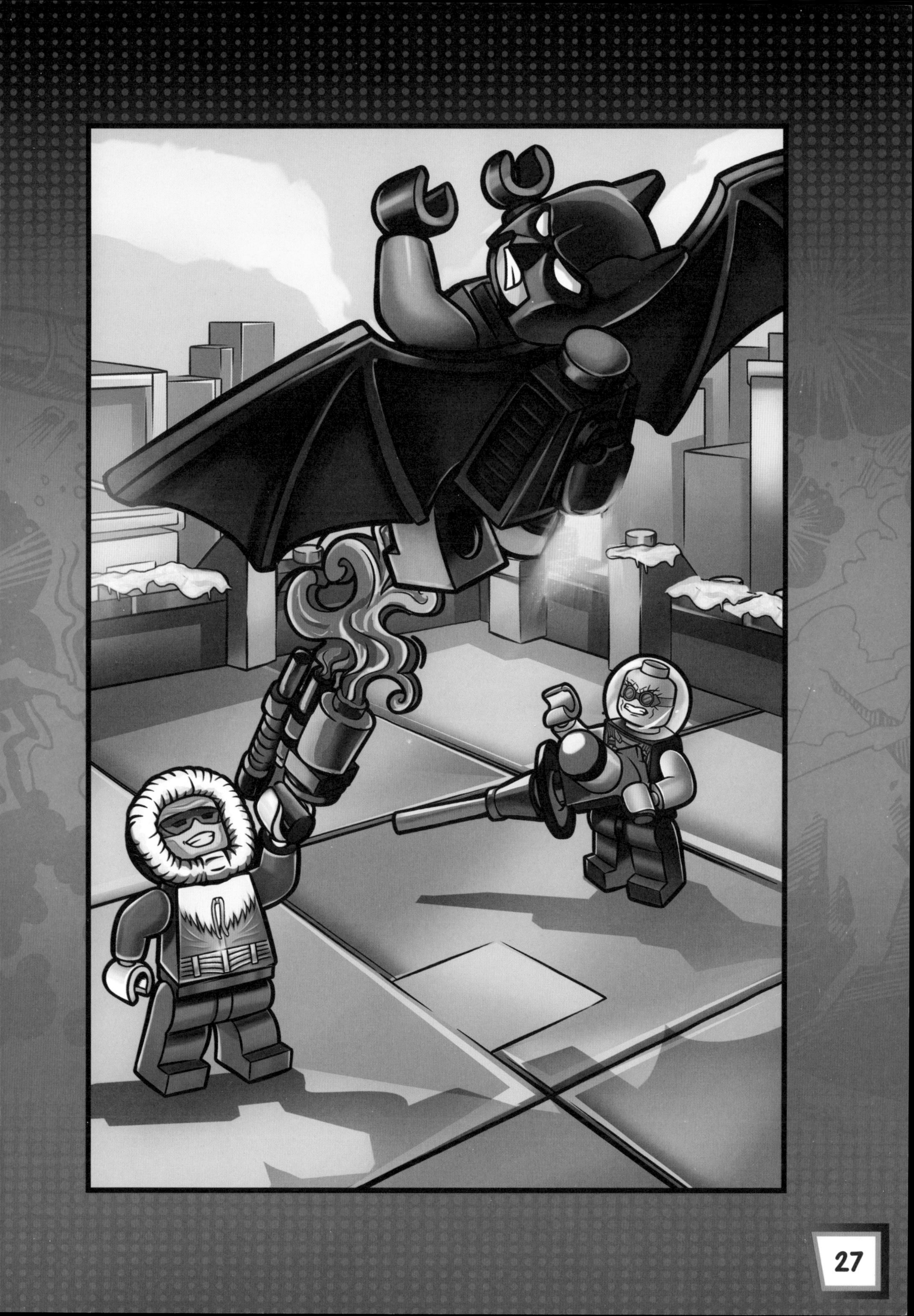

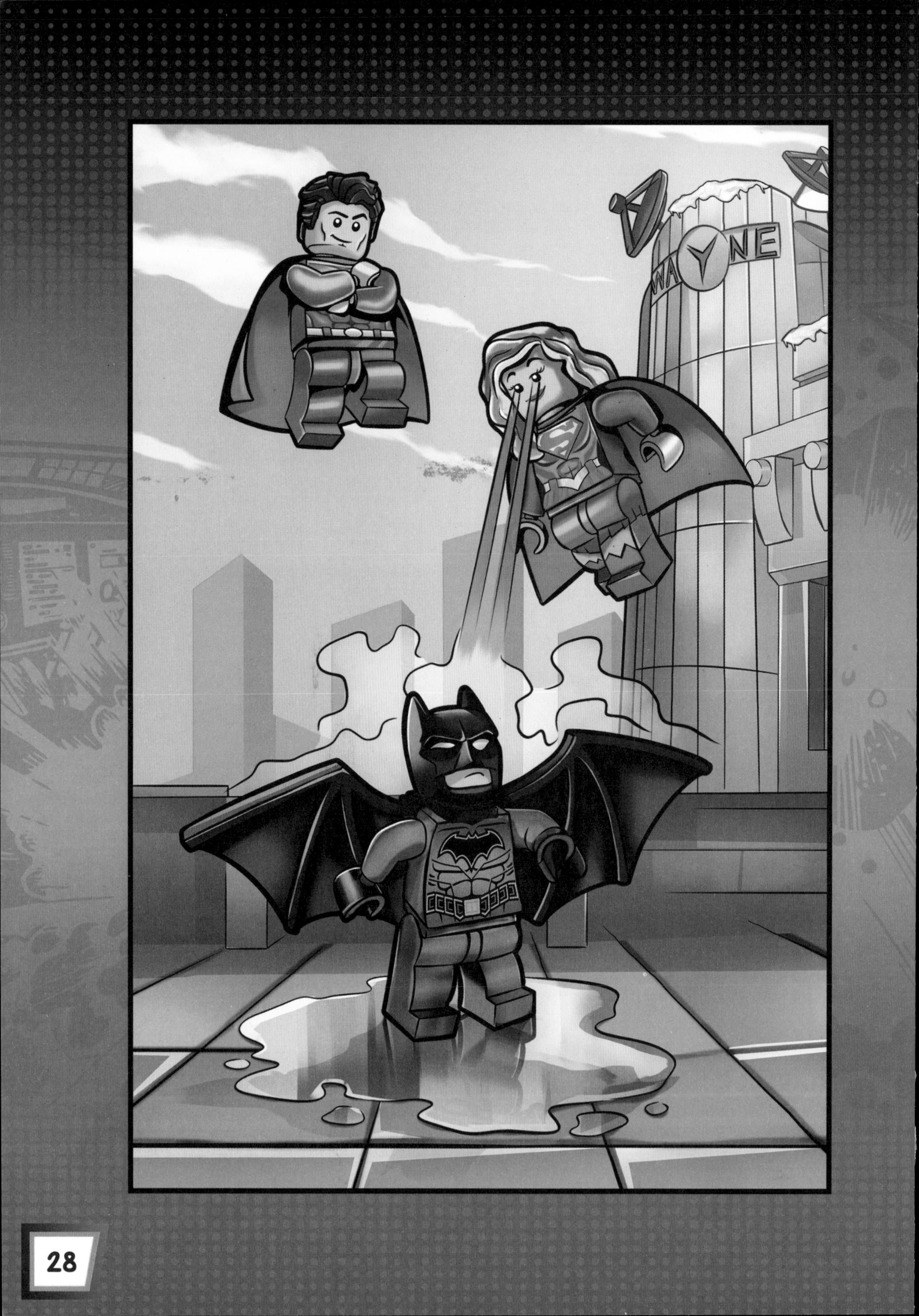

Sure enough, three blurs came zipping toward Batman. One blur was a red-and-gold streak moving across the ground, and the other two were blue-and-red streaks in the sunny sky. A moment later, Supergirl and Superman caught Batman and lowered him to the ground. The Flash was waiting.

"Happy to help, as always," said Superman while Supergirl used her heat vision to melt the ice off Batman.

"This is Captain Cold, isn't it?" The Flash asked.

Batman held out a hand to slow The Flash down. "He's teamed up with Mr. Freeze, Flash. The whole city is in danger if the temperature keeps dropping like this." Batman shivered. "We need a plan. Can you get them away from those dishes?"

"You bet!" yelled The Flash. "Watch this!" He ran straight up the side of the tower. "Hey, icicle boy!" he shouted as he zoomed in circles around the balcony. "Bet you can't cool *my* heels!"

Mr. Freeze snarled, and Captain Cold started firing wildly at The Flash. "Hold still!" shouted Cold.

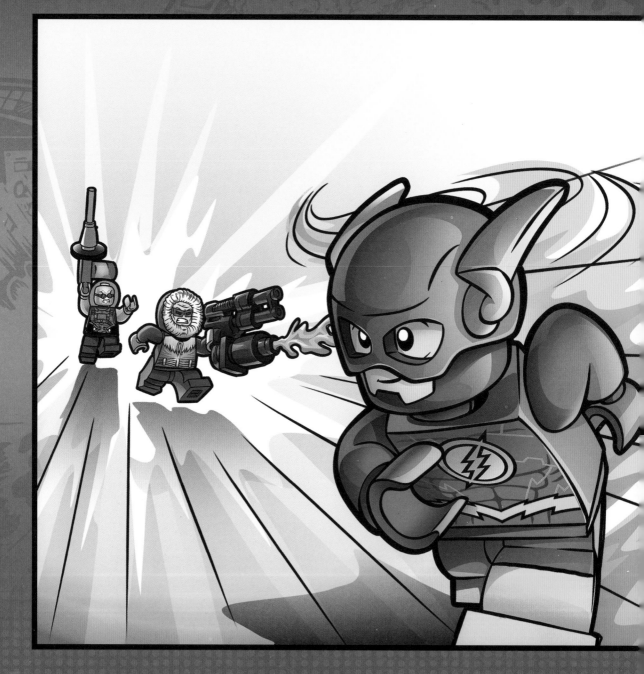

"Not a chance!" The Flash called over his
shoulder as he ran into the building. Captain
Cold and Mr. Freeze followed him through the
door, yelling and firing their freeze rays.

"Good work, Flash," Batman said into his
communicator. Then he turned to Superman and
Supergirl. "I need those rays offline right away."

"No problem," said Superman. He and
Supergirl flew up the side of the tower.

Batman looked around. "The temperature
is dropping too fast," he muttered to himself.
"Everyone will start to freeze, even if we turn off
those rays. There's got to be a way to warm the
city up faster." Then he had an idea. He activated
his communicator again. "Superman, Supergirl,"
he said. "Bring those glass dishes down to me."

At the top of the tower, Supergirl looked up from where she had just punched a dish down to a bunch of bricks. "Uh," she said, "are pieces okay?"

Batman smiled. "Pieces are even better."

In less than a minute, Superman and Supergirl had broken all four dishes, and Batman was standing in front of a large pile of freeze-ray chunks. He got to work assembling a huge circle of clear glass bricks on the ground.

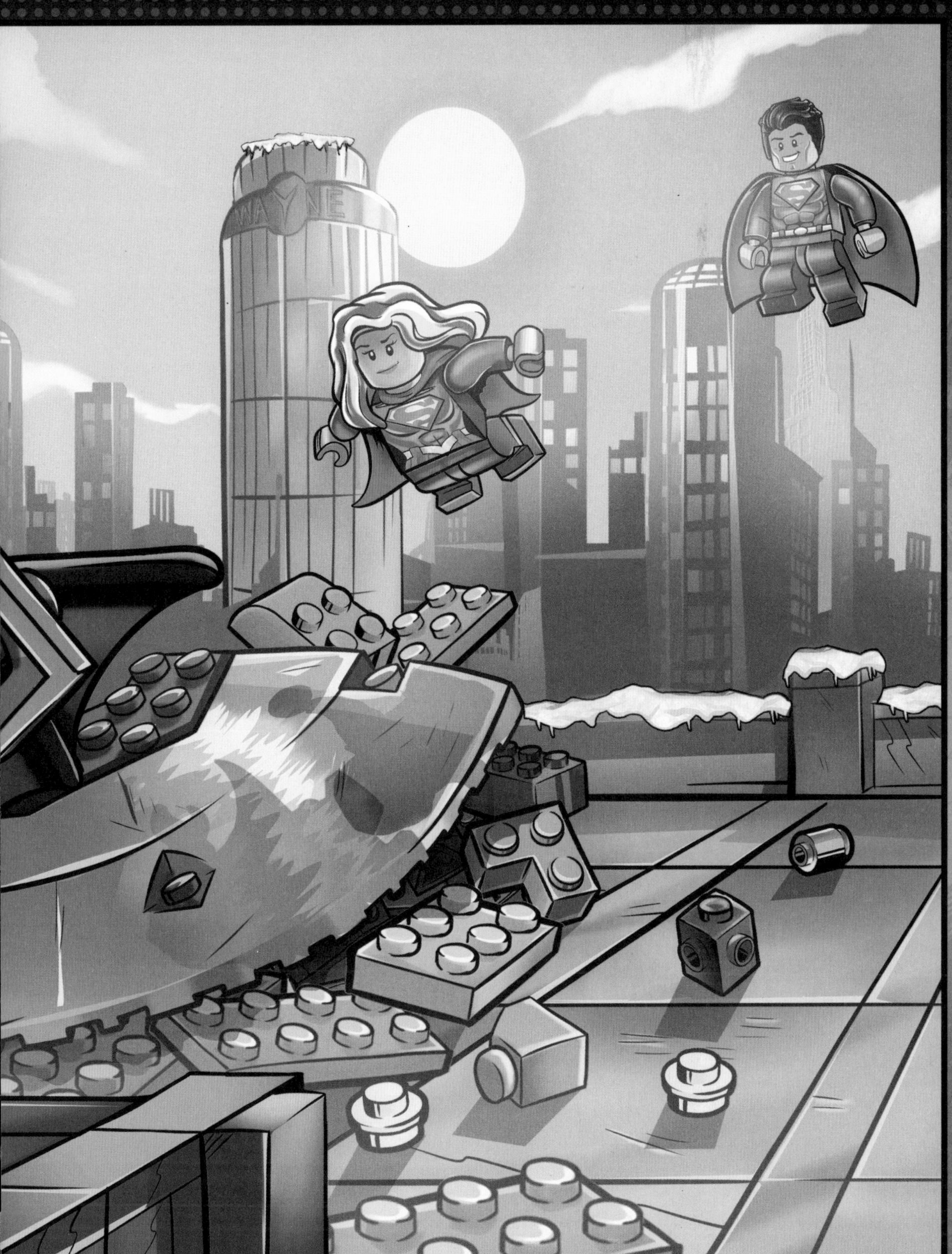
WAYNE

Superman hovered nearby.

Batman fit the last piece into place. Can you and Supergirl fly this up over the city?"

Supergirl lifted one side of the disc. "It looks like . . ."

"A magnifying glass!" Superman finished. "I knew you'd think of something, Batman. Come on, Supergirl!"

Together, Superman and Supergirl lifted the magnifying glass into the air. The strong sunlight shot through the glass and focused a beam of heat onto the ground. The heat began to melt the snow. They swept the beam back and forth over the city.

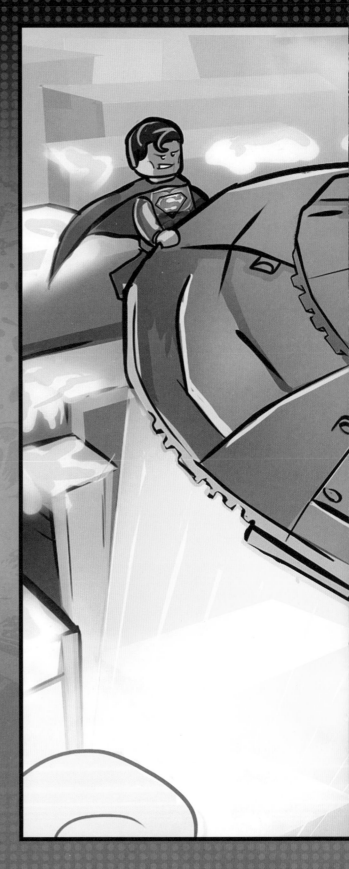

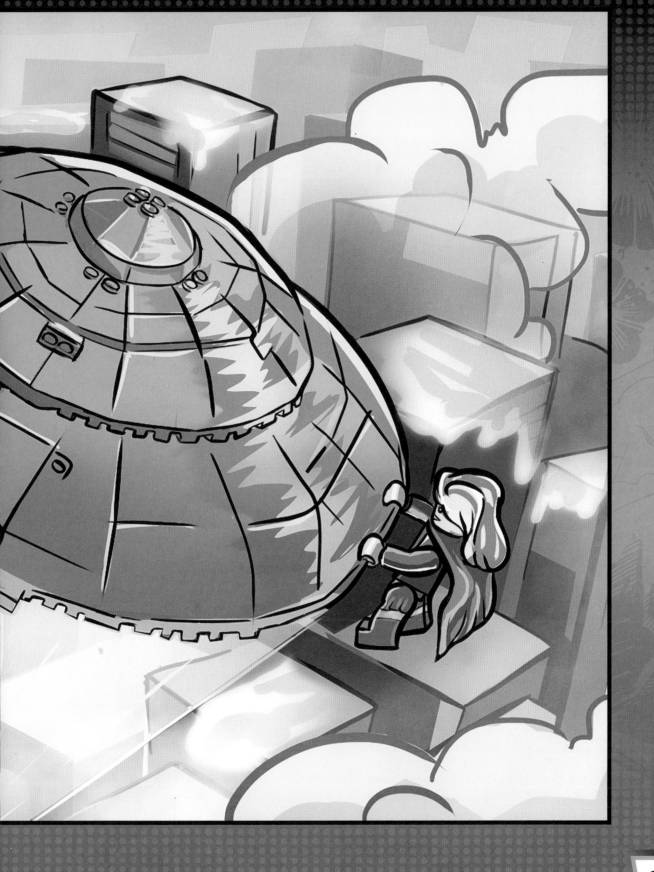

Meanwhile, Batman headed into the Wayne Industries lobby. There he saw Captain Cold and Mr. Freeze tied up securely with the wires and hoses from the freeze rays. Next to them was The Flash, speed-painting a portrait of the two embarrassed Super-Villains.

"Batman, you're just in time!" said The Flash happily. "This is for you to hang in the Batcave. You know, the next time you want to chill out."

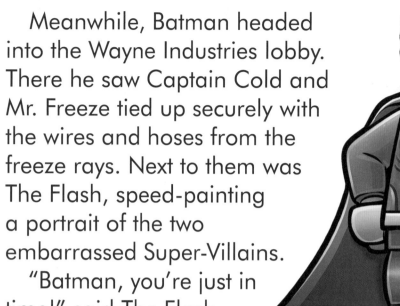

CLOWN SCHOOL

Based on the story by Liz Marsham

The Joker is on the loose, and Batman can't find the criminal clown anywhere! He's running out of ideas and needs a clue. When he sees an ad for a new Clown School, Batman knows it has to be The Joker's funny business! So Batman asks his friend Supergirl to go undercover! Can Batman and Supergirl teach The Joker a lesson he'll never forget?

37

The Joker had escaped from Arkham Asylum two days before, and Batman needed to find him before he caused any trouble! He sat at the Batcomputer, searching through the local news for clues.

Batman sighed and clicked through to the classified ads from the previous day's *Gotham Gazette*, not expecting to see anything. Then he snapped to attention. Among the job ads and furniture for sale, he saw:

Beneath the ad was an address for a warehouse on the edge of town. Batman checked the clock.

He switched on his Justice League communicator. "Batman calling Supergirl," he said. "Are you there, Supergirl?"

"Of course!" Supergirl responded immediately. "And it's not even a school day! What do you need?"

"I need you to go undercover at a clown college for me." Batman said. "I suspect it's being run by The Joker."

"Oh!" Supergirl replied. "That sounds like fun, too! I'll be right there."

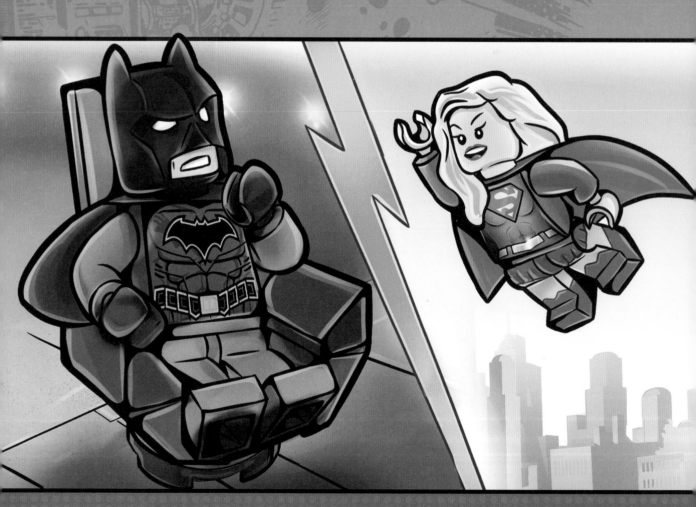

A little while later, Batman and Supergirl crouched on a rooftop across the street from the clown school. Supergirl was dressed in a T-shirt and leggings and had her hair pulled back so that no one would recognize her.

"All right," Batman said, "the auditions are about to start. If you see The Joker, try to find out what he's planning. I'll be right here if you need me."

Supergirl entered a small lobby filled with people waiting to audition. One by one, people were called. After half an hour, Supergirl realized something important: none of them were coming back out!

When it was finally Supergirl's turn, she found herself in a large office filled with novelty gags and tricks: chattering teeth, rubber chickens, cream pies, joy buzzers, and giant mallets were piled in every corner. And behind a big desk were The Joker . . . and his partner in crime, Harley Quinn!

Harley looked at Supergirl and said to The Joker, "See, Mr. J? This one looks nice and strong, too! I told ya having more clowns in the gang was a good idea!"

The Joker quickly replied, "AHEM. What my assistant is trying to say is that we have room for one more student in our school. If you pass the audition, that is."

"Yeah, right." Harley laughed. "So make with the clowning, and let's see what you've got."

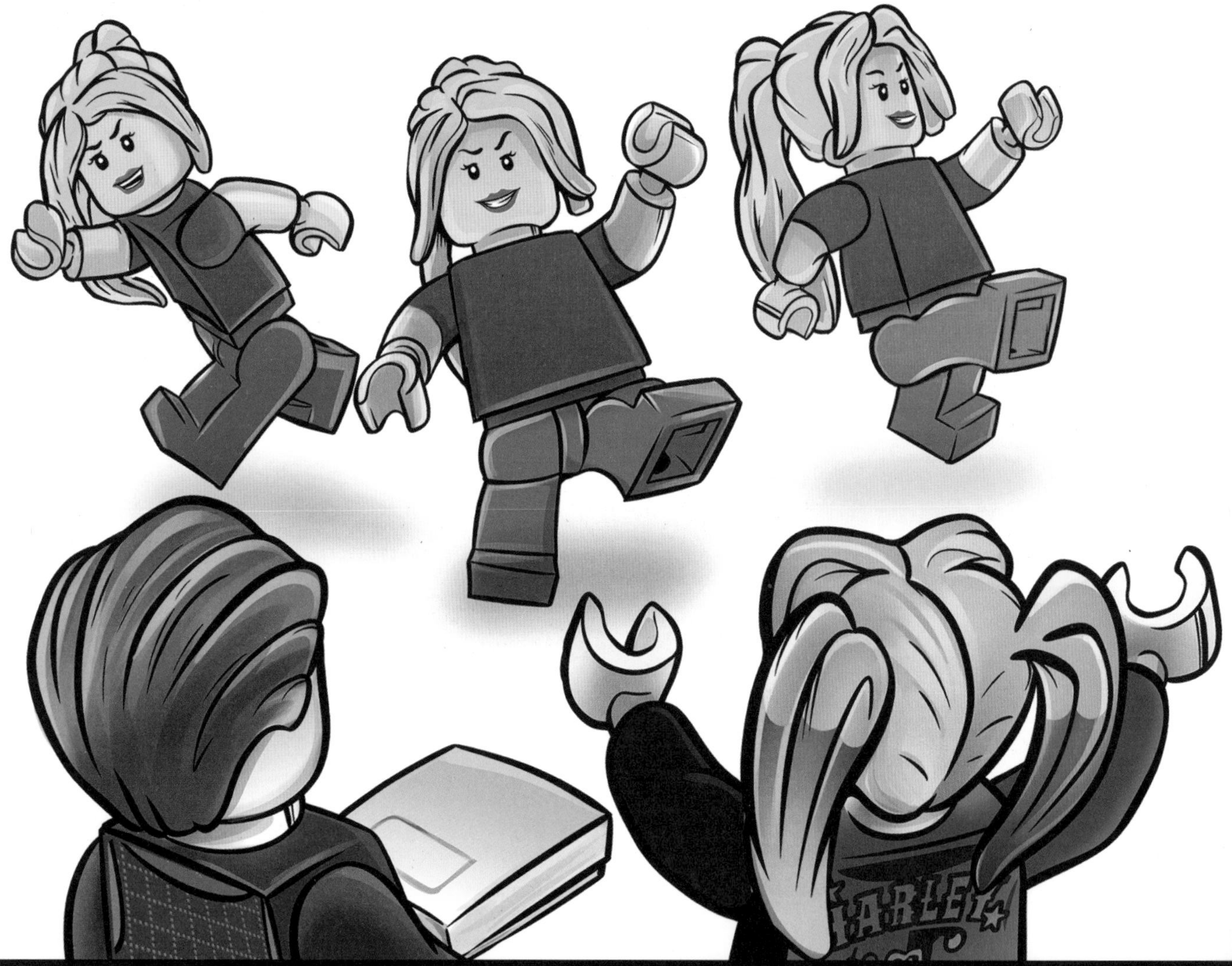

Supergirl straightened up, put her hands on her hips, and launched into a cheer.

"Give me a *P!*" she cheered, waving her arms.

"*P!*" Harley immediately called back at her.

"Give me an *I!*" Supergirl continued, kicking up a leg.

"*I!*" Harley yelled.

"Ay-yi-yi," The Joker said, rolling his eyes.

"Give me an *E!*" called Supergirl, doing a back handspring into a corner of the room.

"*E!*" Harley shouted.

"What's that spell?" asked Supergirl, straightening up again.

"PIE!" Harley shouted at the top of her lungs.

"If you insist!" said Supergirl, and she flung a cream pie right into Harley's face.

The Joker burst out laughing. "You're okay, kid!"
"And those moves weren't bad, either," Harley added, wiping the pie off her face.

Harley and The Joker showed Supergirl through a heavy door at the back of the office, which led to the main floor of the warehouse. Supergirl stopped short in surprise. There was a huge green-and-purple machine in the middle of the warehouse floor. Dozens of dazed-looking people swarmed the machine. Every one of them was wearing clown makeup.

"Ah, yes," said The Joker, sensing Supergirl's hesitation. "This is our . . . term project. It'll make a lot more sense once you try on the school uniform. Right this way."

He pushed Supergirl to where Harley waited with a tub of white makeup. Supergirl had just enough time to read the label—HAPPY THOUGHTS—before she felt the cold greasepaint being slathered over her face.

"See?" said Harley, leaning down to look in her eyes. "Isn't that better? Now get a move on! That laughing gas isn't going to make itself, you know!"

"Batman!" she hissed into her earpiece. "You were right! The Joker and Harley set this place up to recruit new gang members, and they're building a dangerous device. They have this makeup that I think makes people follow their orders, but I guess I'm immune."

"Be very careful, Supergirl," Batman said into her ear.

"So are you if you come in here!" Supergirl pointed out. She scanned the warehouse, spotting one of the water pipes. "Never mind. I found a way to even the score."

Supergirl's eyes turned red, and her heat vision blasted the water pipe. With a *FWOOSH,* the pipe burst, soaking everyone in the warehouse. The makeup was washed away in the flood, revealing several very confused people underneath.

Suddenly, Batman crashed through one
of the warehouse windows. He slammed into
Harley and The Joker, knocking them into
a puddle, where they lay on their backs,
grumbling. After a few seconds, Supergirl and
Batman approached and offered their hands.

"Looks like you could use some help getting up, Joker," said Batman.

The Joker and Harley grinned at each other. As soon as they were back on their feet, they were going to fight! They reached out their hands to the Super Heroes.

ZAP! The joy buzzers hidden in Batman's and Supergirl's palms shocked the Super-Villains. The Joker and Harley fell back, dazed.

"It looks like I taught you well!" The Joker admitted. "Class dismissed!"

TRICK OR THIEF?

Based on the story by Liz Marsham

Even Super Heroes get scared sometimes! When a mysterious house appears out of thin air, Halloween gets a little too spooky for The Flash. He calls Batman and Batgirl to help him investigate. His friends are there for him faster than you can say "Trick or treat!" Together, they'll find out if the creepy mansion is really haunted or just a horrible Halloween hoax!

It was Halloween in Central City, the home of The Flash! Kids in costumes ran all over the city, trick-or-treating. A group of friends in a quiet neighborhood already had bags full of candy, but they remembered there was a house at the end of their block that they hadn't been to yet.

The old house they remembered was gone! In its place was a big, creepy mansion. The kids thought it was weird that this dusty old mansion had popped up out of nowhere. But they wanted candy, so they walked up to the front door. Then, slowly, the doorknob started to turn—

"AAAAAAH!" the kids screamed, and they ran away.

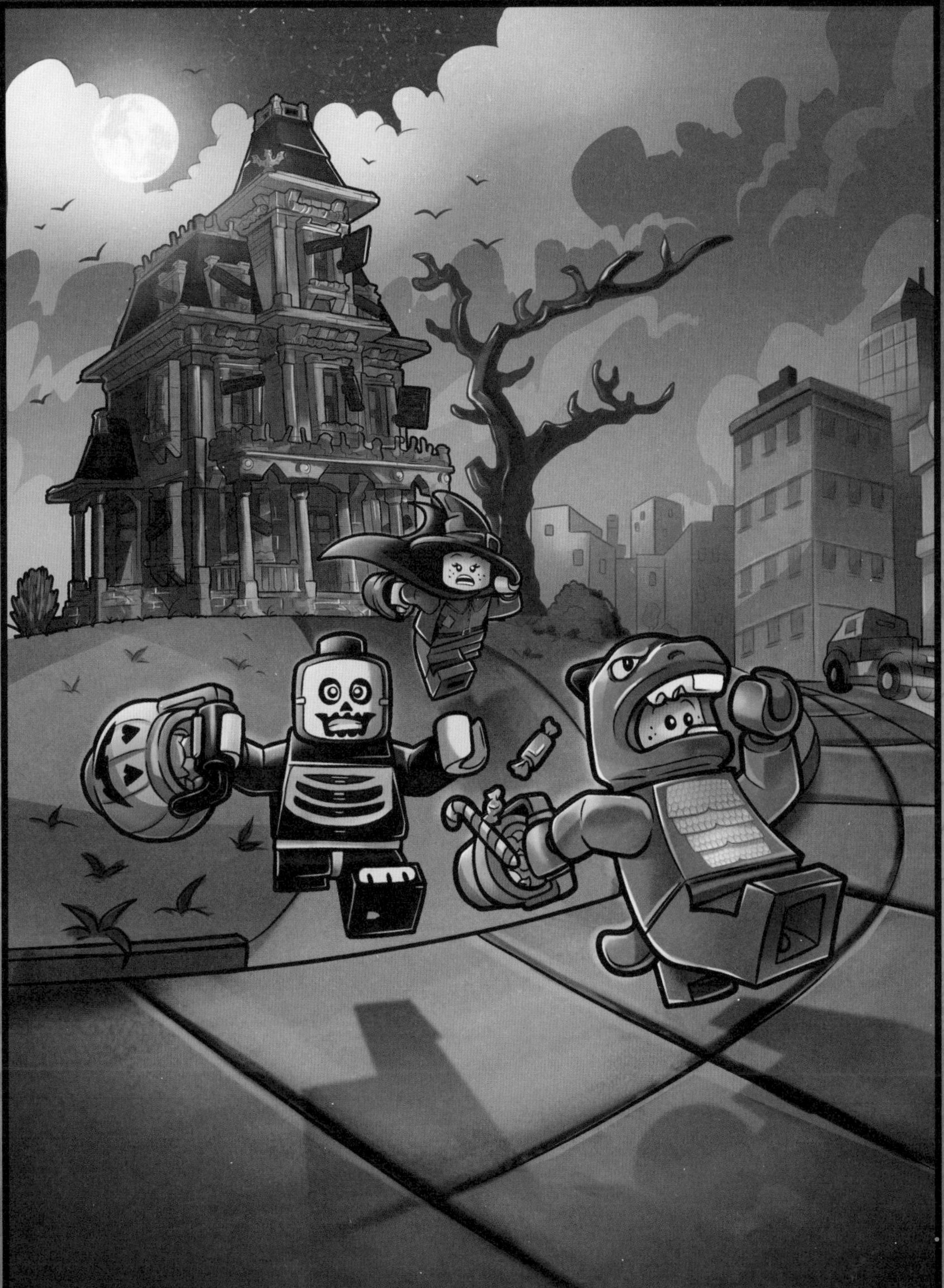

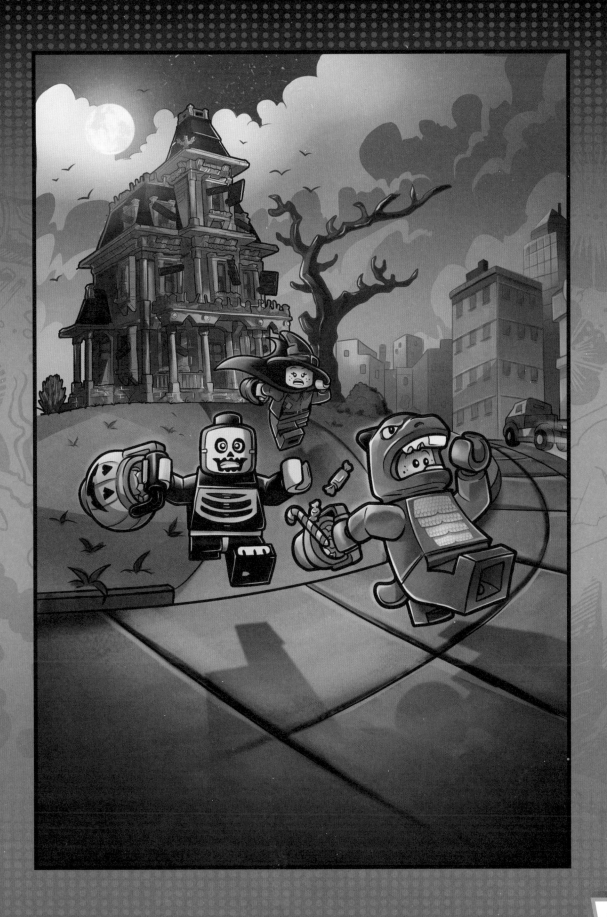

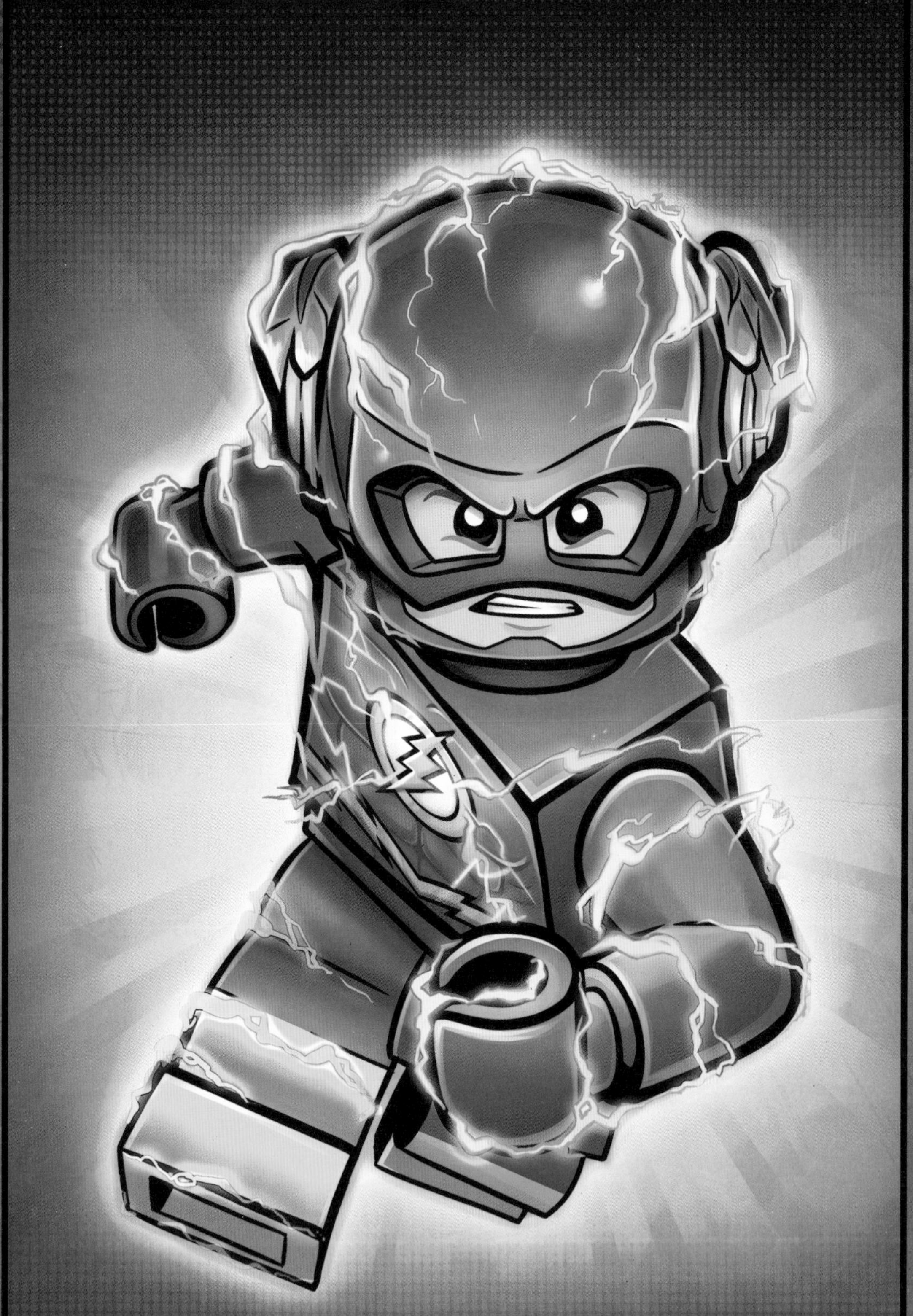

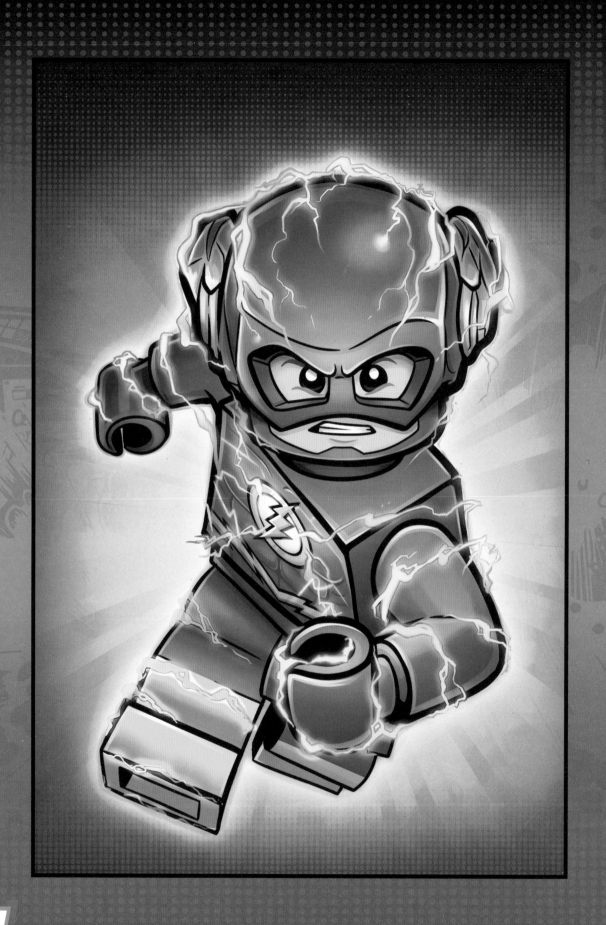

As they ran down the street, they passed a man in costume—it was The Flash! But he wasn't trick-or-treating. He was always dressed like that.

"Wow, I know Halloween is scary, but those kids seem really scared!" he thought. He looked at the old mansion the kids were running from.

He walked up to the front door of the mansion and looked around.

"Well," he said, hopping from foot to foot, "this sure is a big, scary old house. Hmm . . . maybe I shouldn't go in alone." He tapped his Justice League communicator, a special earpiece he had that let him talk to his Super Hero friends. "Hey, uh, does anyone want to come to Central City to see a big, creepy mansion that seems to have come out of nowhere?"

"Do I ever!" Batgirl responded.

"I admit, I am also . . . interested," said Batman.

"Oh, yeah, Batman, this is totally your kind of place!" The Flash said.

"We'll be right there," Batgirl answered.

Within minutes, the Super Heroes were in the Batwing and on their way to Central City!

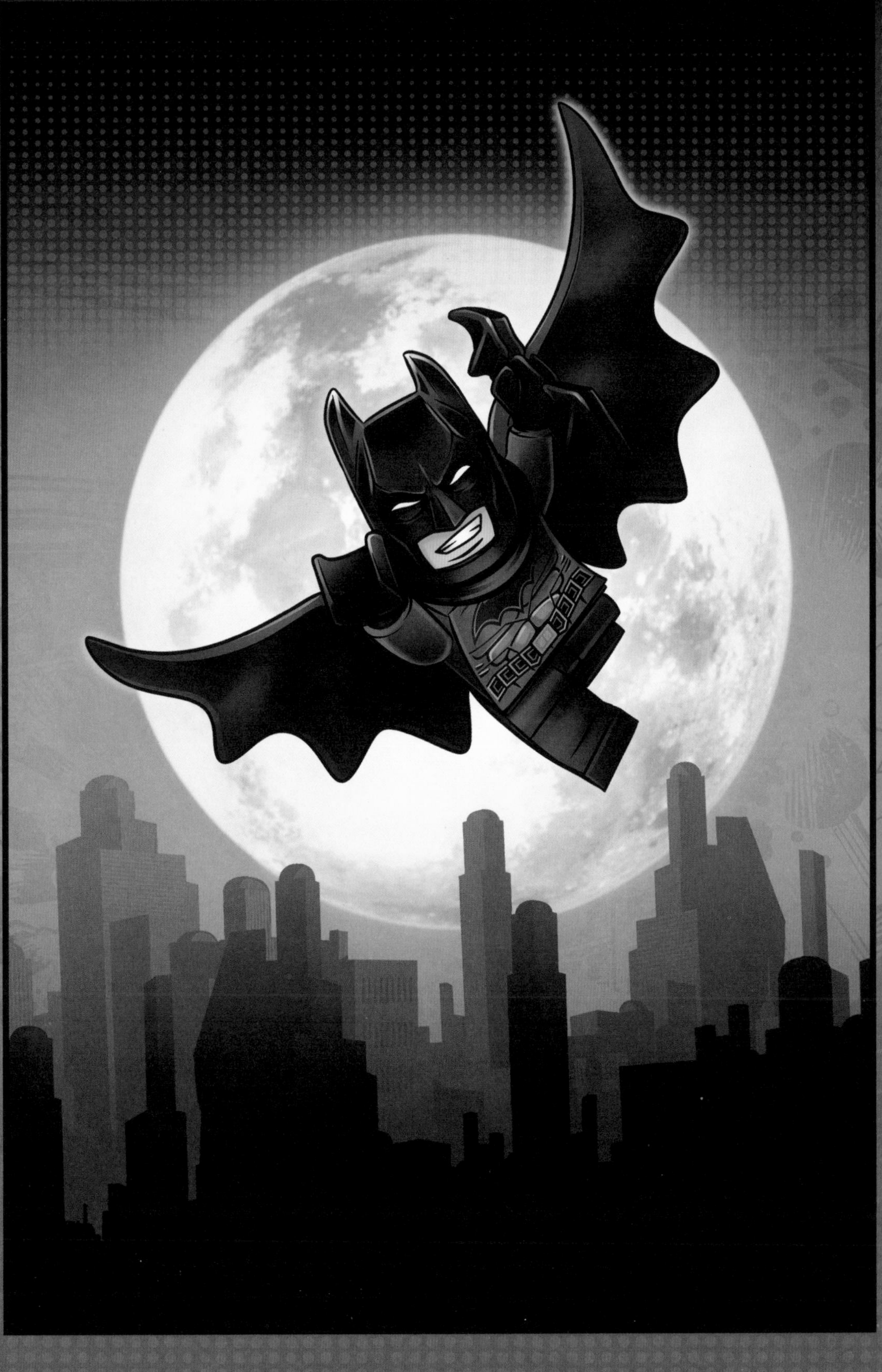

With his friends behind him, The Flash slowly opened the mansion door. The house was full of dusty furniture and had cobwebs on the ceiling. There were tattered old books on bookcases. Batman and Batgirl crept into the room, followed by The Flash.

Batman drew a line through the dust on a coffee table. "This place looks really old. . . ."

Just then, a rush of air moved through the room, and *SLAM!* The front door shut behind them.

"Try to be quiet, Flash," said Batgirl.

"I didn't slam that door!" The Flash replied.

"Well, it wasn't me," Batgirl said.

"And it wasn't me," said Batman.

"Okay . . . ," The Flash said, "then I think it's clear that we are standing inside a haunted house!"

"Flash," Batman barked, "there's no such thing as ghosts."

"But someone wants us to think this house is haunted," added Batgirl, pulling out her phone.

There was another rush of air. Book after book came flying off one of the shelves and landed on the floor.

"YAH!" yelped The Flash, jumping into Batman's arms.

"Well, while you were busy not being scared," said Batgirl with a giggle, "I was recording."

Batgirl held up her phone.

"You recorded that?" The Flash hopped off Batman, who adjusted his cape.

"Well, yeah," Batgirl replied. "I think I got a good video of the bookshelf, too. Let's see." She tapped on her phone a few times to rewind the footage. "Aha!"

Batman and The Flash looked over Batgirl's shoulders at the video. She paused it just before the books fell off the shelf. There was an orange blur in the video.

"Look how fast that's moving," murmured Batgirl. "What is it?"

"Not 'what'—'who'! That's a speedster!" The Flash said. "So that's how this house was built so fast."

"And now they're using their super-speed to make the house seem haunted!" finished Batgirl. "But why?"

The Flash clapped his hands decisively. "Let's catch 'em quick so we can ask 'em!"

The Super Heroes got together and whispered a plan to one another. After a few minutes, they started walking to the door. . . .

"Too bad we couldn't catch that ghost!" Batgirl called back over her shoulder.

"Yeah, guess we'll just have to give up!" The Flash yelled.

"Oh!" Batman said, very loudly. "Yes! It is a shame that we could not bring this bad-guy ghost to justice!"

Batgirl rolled her eyes at the Caped Crusader and pulled the door shut behind her.

A few seconds passed in the empty room. Then a rush of air and a blur moved toward the door. As it passed over the fallen books, there was a *CLICK* and a *WHOOSH*. Books flew into the air, and then someone was swinging upside down from the ceiling!

BANG! The front door burst open, and the Super Heroes ran in. In the main room, hanging by one ankle from a booby trap that the Super Heroes had secretly set, was one of the Justice League's enemies: The Cheetah! She was half woman, half cheetah, with both super-strength and super-speed.

"Cheetah," Batman said sternly, "what are you up to in this house?"

The Cheetah sighed. "I needed someplace safe to hide all"—she paused—"my stuff."

"You mean all your stolen loot?" Batgirl corrected.

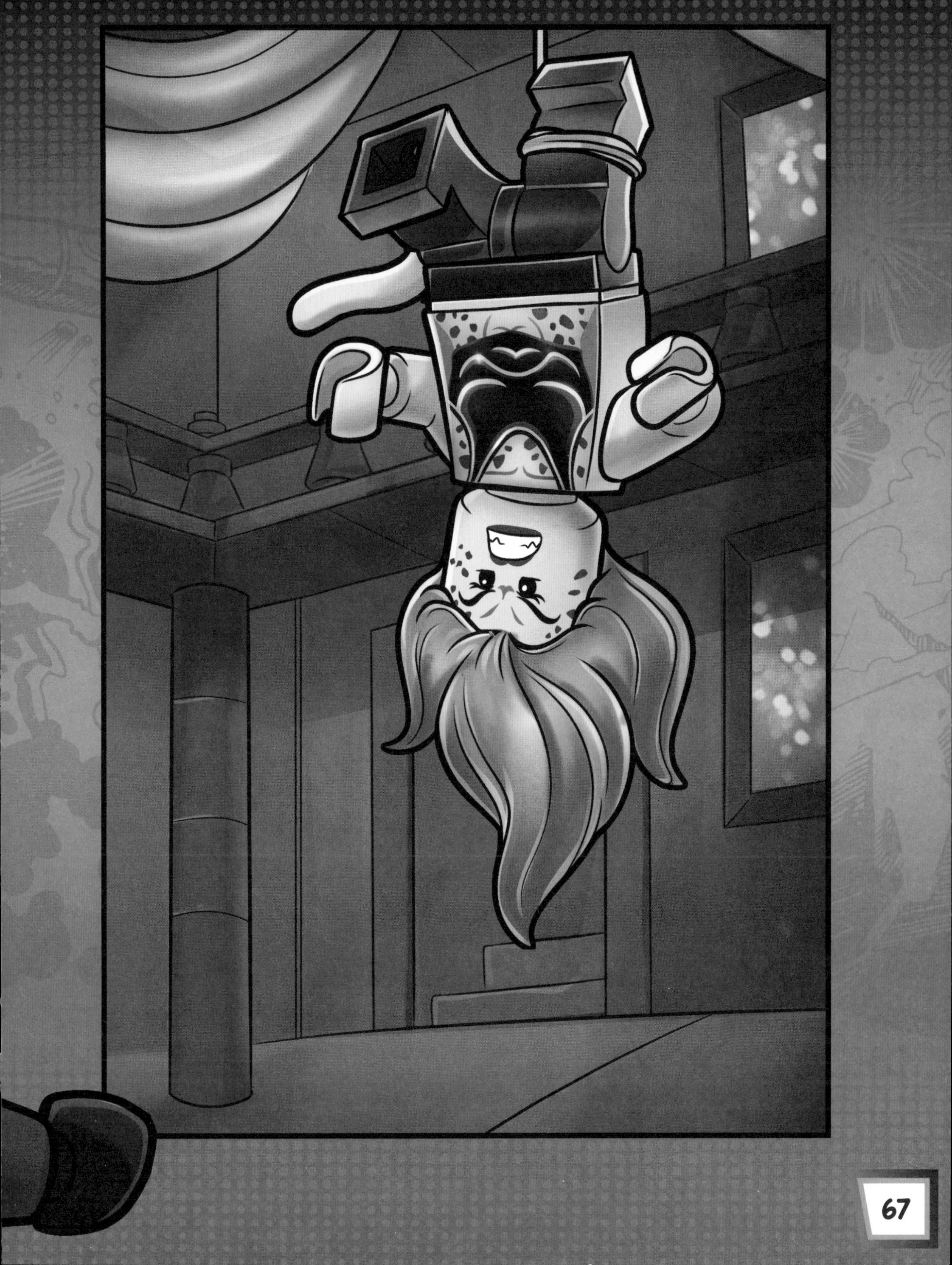

"Yes, fine!" The Cheetah snarled. "So I built the scariest-looking house I could. If everyone thought it was haunted, they would stay away. No one was supposed to come here!" She frowned at them. "How did you even set this trap? I was watching you. You had no time!"

"Cheetah," said The Flash proudly, "you may be as spooky as a ghost. But no one is faster than The Flash!"

GROCERY STORE GHOSTS

Based on the story by Liz Marsham

Things are far from chill at the grocery store. The Flash gets called in to investigate a series of strange robberies! The clues are bizarre! And the items stolen are even stranger! The Flash is stumped—and a little spooked! He calls his friends Superman and Supergirl to help get to the bottom of the weird crimes. But can they find the bad guy behind the crimes? Or will the bad guy find them first?

It was early in the morning, but The Flash was already hard at work. A Central City grocery store had been robbed overnight!

The Flash was pointing to some puddles of water as he talked to the store manager.

"This is really the only clue?"

The manager shrugged. "Those," she said, "and that." She pointed at the spicy food section, where all the shelves had been cleaned out. "Whoever—or whatever—did this? They took everything."

"What do you mean 'whatever'?" asked The Flash.

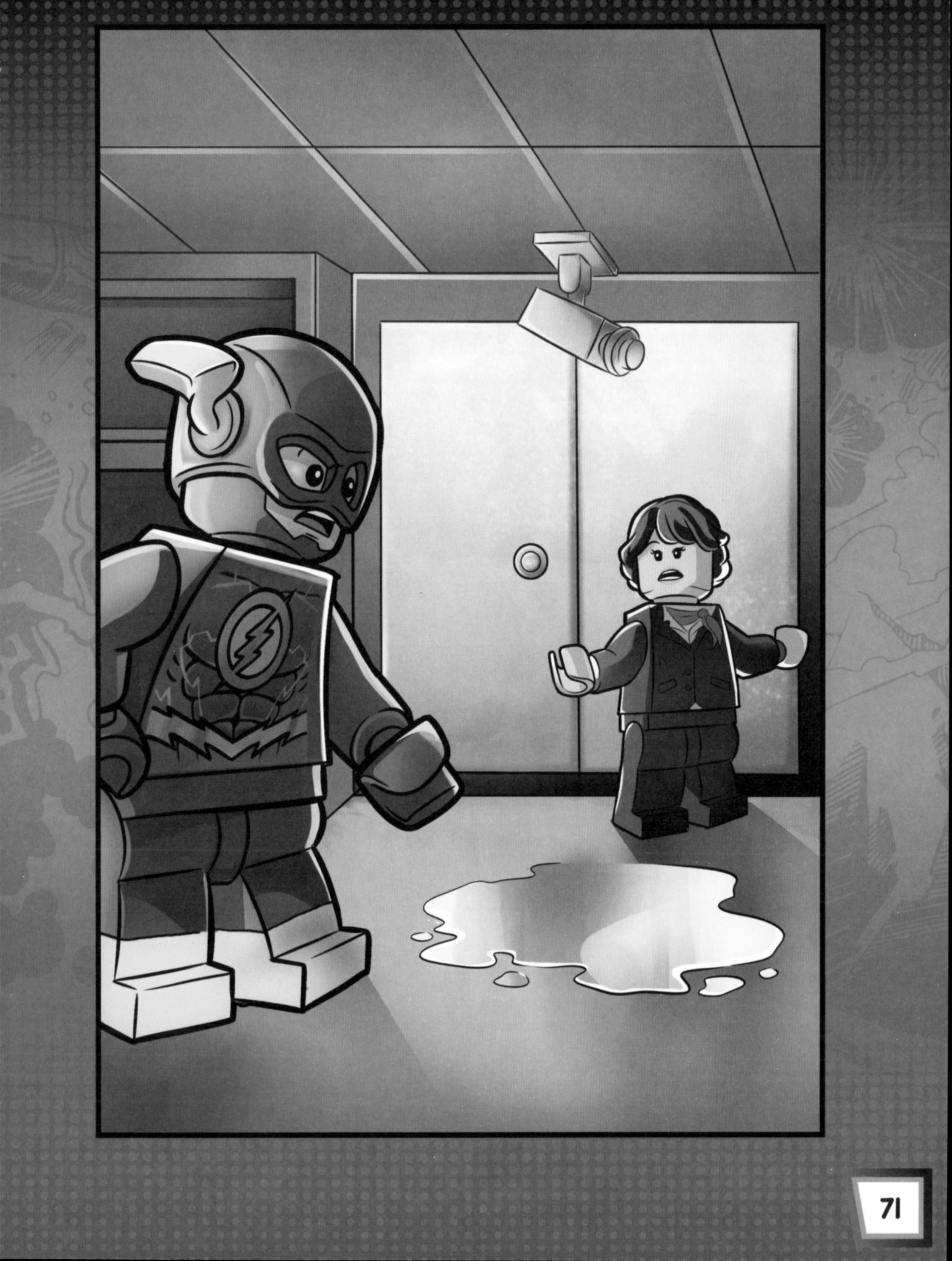

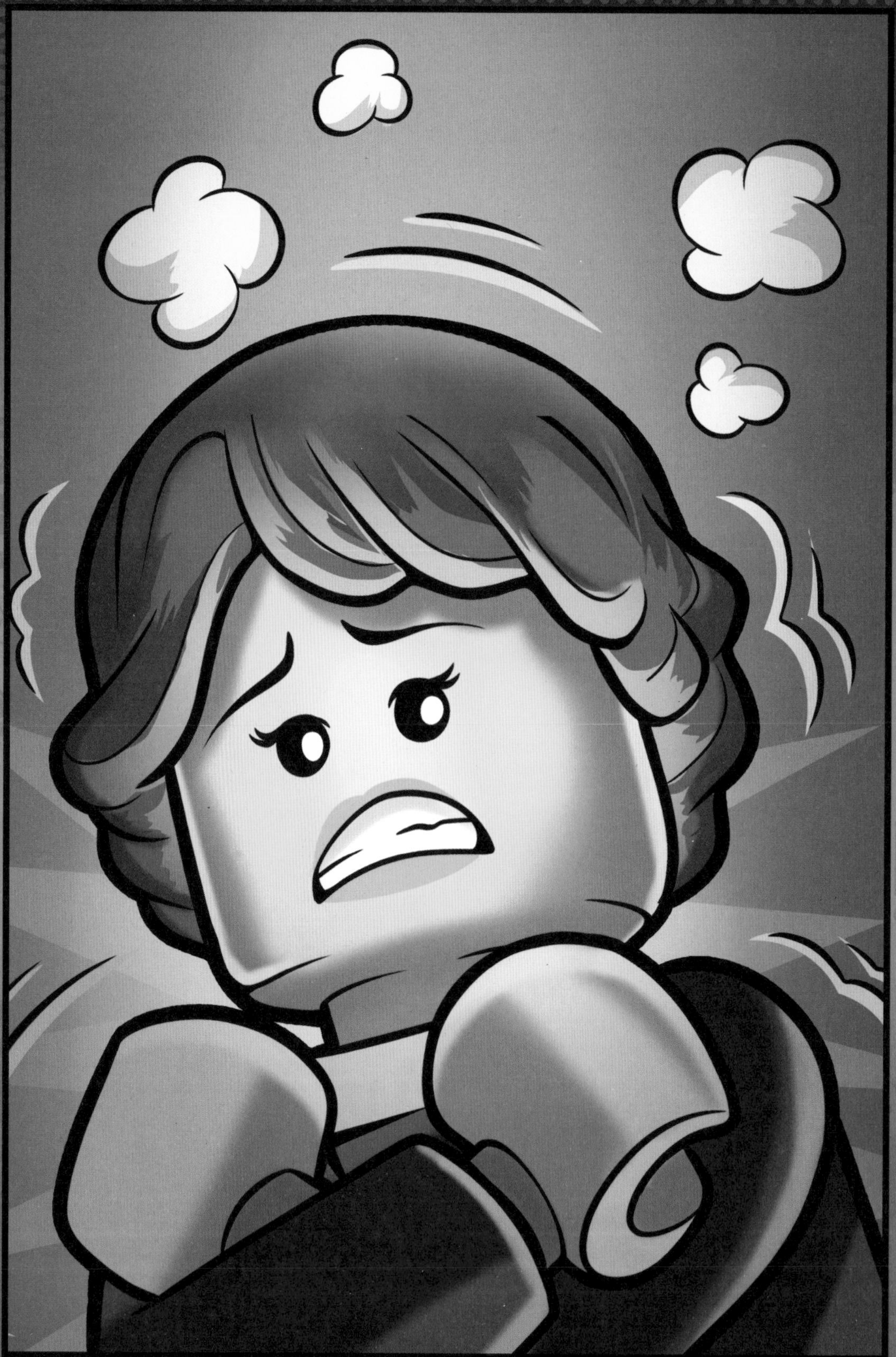

"Well," said the manager nervously, "this is the third grocery store this has happened to. Every time, there's nothing left behind except these weird puddles of water. And the thieves just take all the hot sauce and spicy food. And every time"—she shivered—"when everyone gets to work the next morning, the whole store is freezing!"

"Oh," The Flash said, "it's not normally this cold in here? I thought you just liked it chilly!"

"No!" The manager leaned in, whispering, "Some of us think it may be . . . some sort of gh-gh-ghost!"

Wait. You really think it's a ghost?

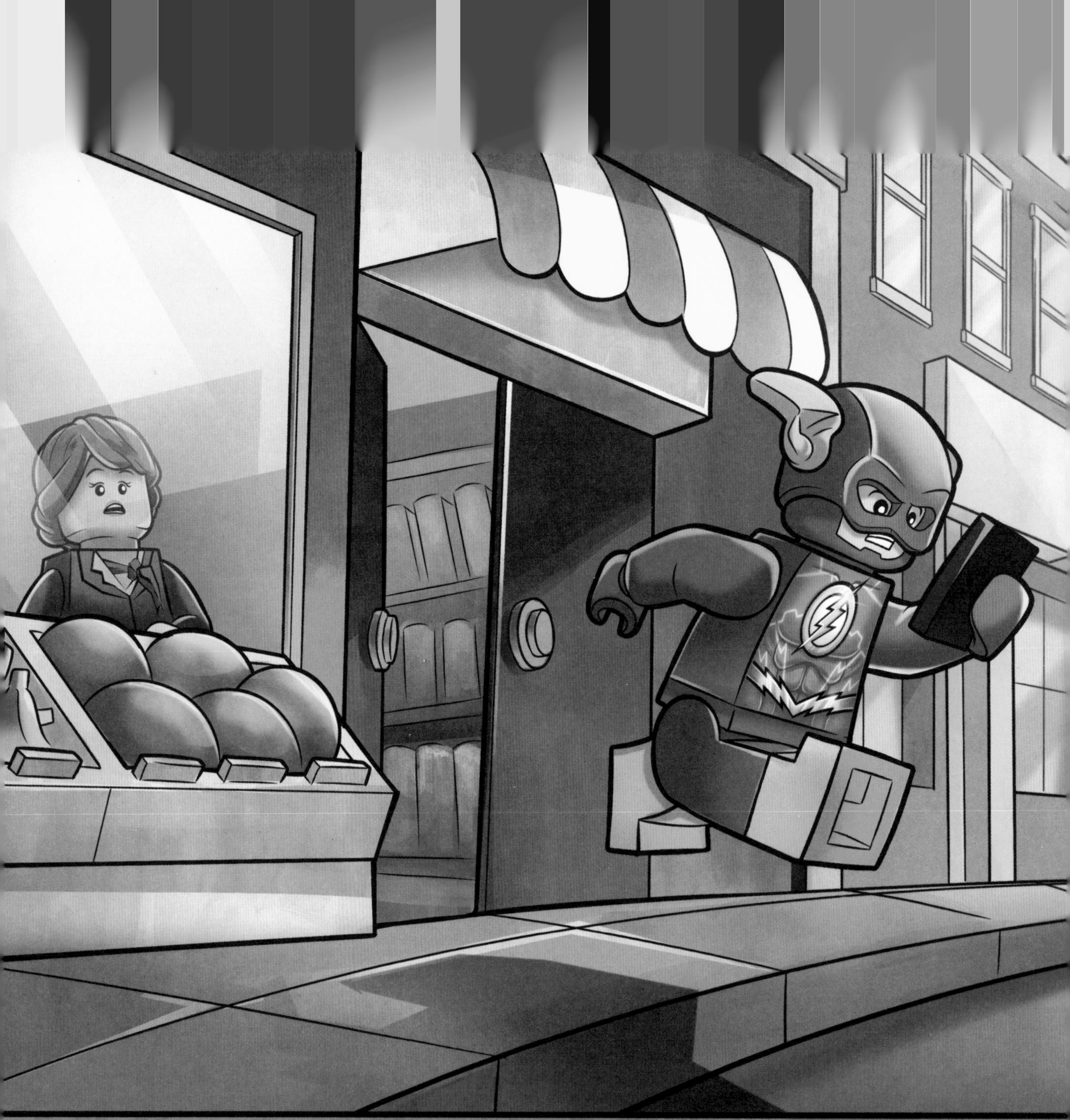

"Hoo, okay," continued The Flash. "Uh . . . be right back." He darted outside and activated his Justice League communicator. "Haunted grocery store! Haunted grocery store!"

"Hello? Flash, is that you?" came Superman's voice.

"Yes! Also . . . haunted grocery store!"

"Neato!" responded Supergirl. "We'll be right there!"

When Superman and Supergirl arrived at the store, The Flash showed them the puddles of water. "See?" he said. "Creepy puddles, missing spicy food, and the air is always chilly. It's a spicy taco ghost!"

"Not necessarily, Flash," said Superman. "Cold can mean lots of things, not just ghosts."

"Yeah, watch!" said Supergirl. She blew a frosty breath at a shelf nearby, turning it into a giant ice cube.

"Exactly." Superman nodded. "Our freeze breath is enough to stop any villain in their tracks. Until it melts, of course. And there's nothing ghostly about it!"

"Wait. Melts," said The Flash. "That's it!" He raced from puddle to puddle, looking up at the store ceiling. "Look! These puddles are all under the security cameras!"

Supergirl flew up to the nearest camera and opened a panel on the side. Water flooded out and splashed right into The Flash's face.

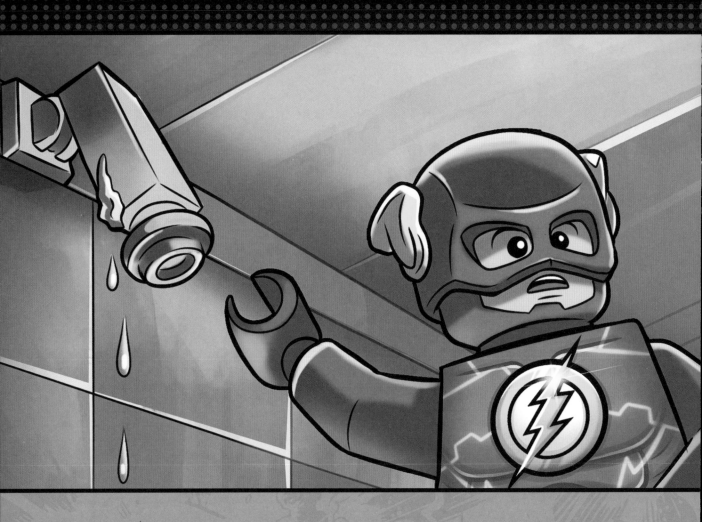

"Ack!" he cried. "It's freezing!"

"No, you were right the first time," Superman said. "It's melting. Someone froze the cameras to make them stop working. And then the ice melted and made these puddles. We're looking for a thief who can control ice!"

That night, Superman, Supergirl, and The Flash hid in the next largest grocery store in the neighborhood. They didn't have to wait long before—

Crackle! Crackle! Crackle! Beams of ice froze the security cameras. Then a familiar figure stepped into the center of the room.

"Frost!" shouted Supergirl, flying down from the shadows. "See, Flash? She's no ghost!"

Frost laughed. "You thought I was a ghost? Ha!" She raised her hands and blasted a wave of frost at Supergirl.

Supergirl dodged the blast. "Ooh, so rude!" she said. Her eyes glowed red, and a ray of heat vision blasted Frost.

"Good idea, Supergirl!" said Superman, striking with his own heat vision.

To the Super Heroes' surprise, Frost didn't seem to mind the heat rays. "Thanks for the pick-me-up," she said with a laugh.

"Wait!" called The Flash. "I just remembered: Frost absorbs heat energy. It makes her stronger, not weaker! That's why she was stealing hot sauce and spicy foods!"

"Aw, come on!" said Frost, turning her ice beam toward The Flash.

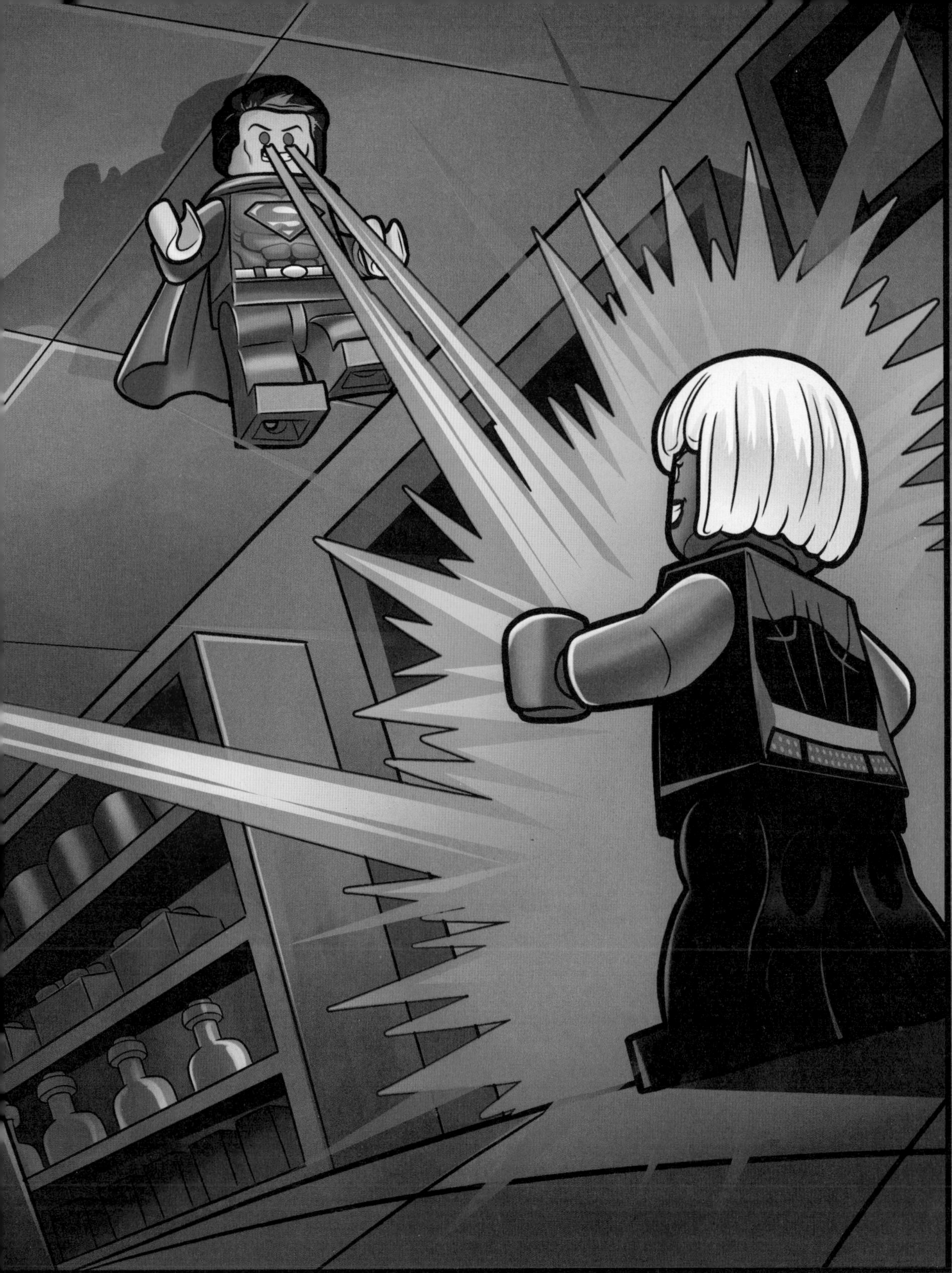

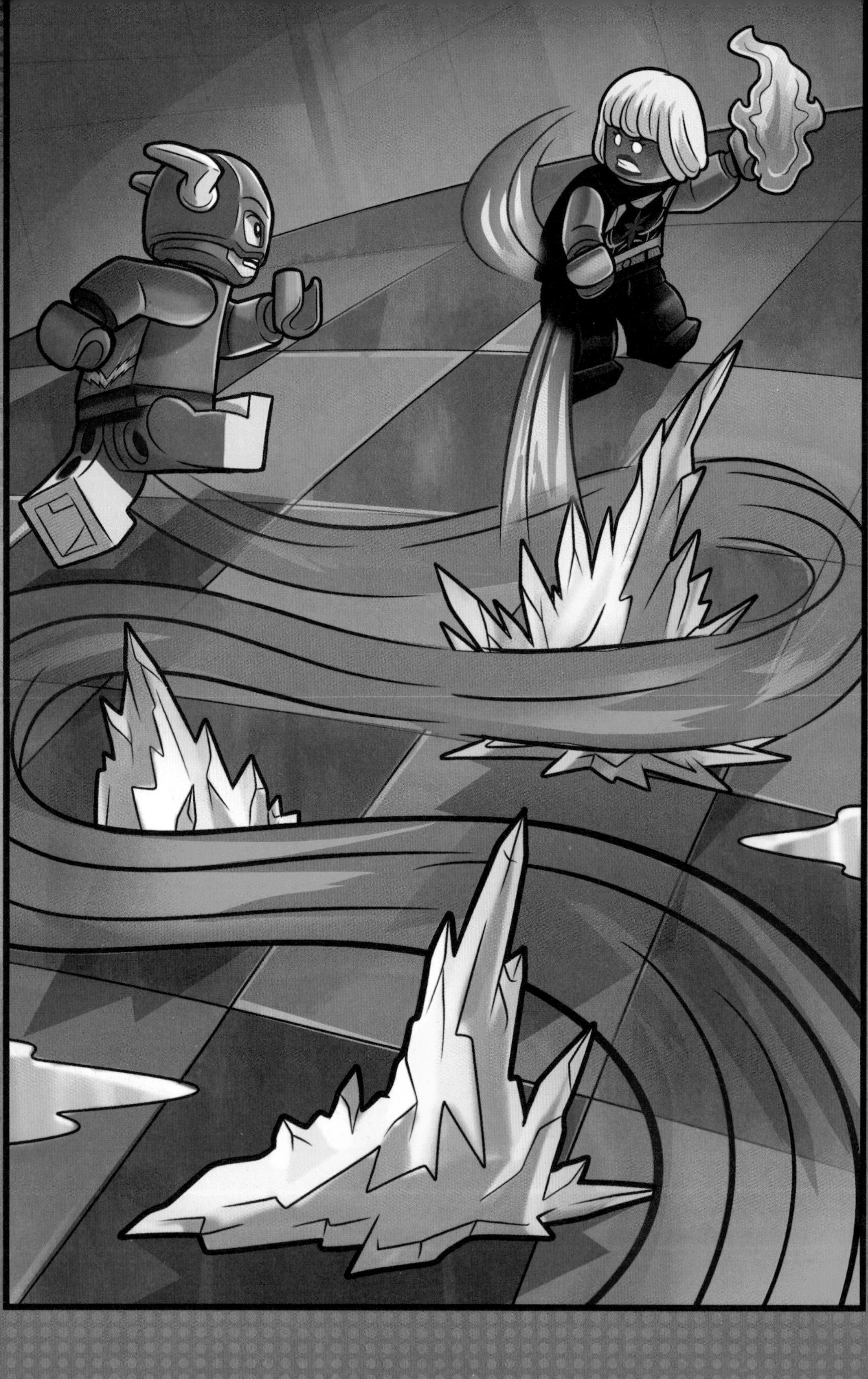

The Flash jumped to the side, and the beam shot by him. "I have an idea to get the heat energy back out of her," he said. "Follow me!"

The Flash ran at Frost, moving from side to side to avoid her ice beams. He ran around her, faster and faster, spinning her in circles.

Frost stood on her feet, dizzy, holding her head with one hand. With the other hand, she tried to fire her ice beams, but she was so dizzy that her aim was terrible. Her ice blasts fired all around the room.

Superman and Supergirl flew down, knocking Frost off-balance so she fell to her knees. Then The Flash grabbed the ice blocks. Before Frost could blink, he piled them all around her.

"Ugh," grumbled Frost, "you are the worst."

"Hey, don't be like that." The Flash chuckled. "Maybe being in jail will give you time to warm up to me."

A Day at the Museum

Based on the story by Liz Marsham

A gang of ghosts is attacking The Flash Museum—but what would ghosts need in a Super Hero museum? Batman and his friends want to get inside for some answers! But first they need a plan to slip past these spooky visitors! If they work together, can they find out what's behind the attack—and what's under those sheets? Even if the ghosts aren't real, the danger is!

Batgirl, Batman, Superman, Supergirl, and The Flash were crouched behind the huge statue of The Flash in front of The Flash Museum. The museum was in the hero's home of Central City and contained trophies from his past adventures.

"I gotta admit, Flash," whispered Batgirl, "when you said your museum was being attacked by ghosts, I had my doubts."

Dozens of white-sheeted figures were climbing all over the outside of the museum.

"And they're trying to get inside," added Batman. "If they succeed, they could steal—"

"The Cosmic Treadmill!" The Flash looked alarmed. "I built that to travel through time."

"Let's find out!" Supergirl said as she and Superman took off for the roof.

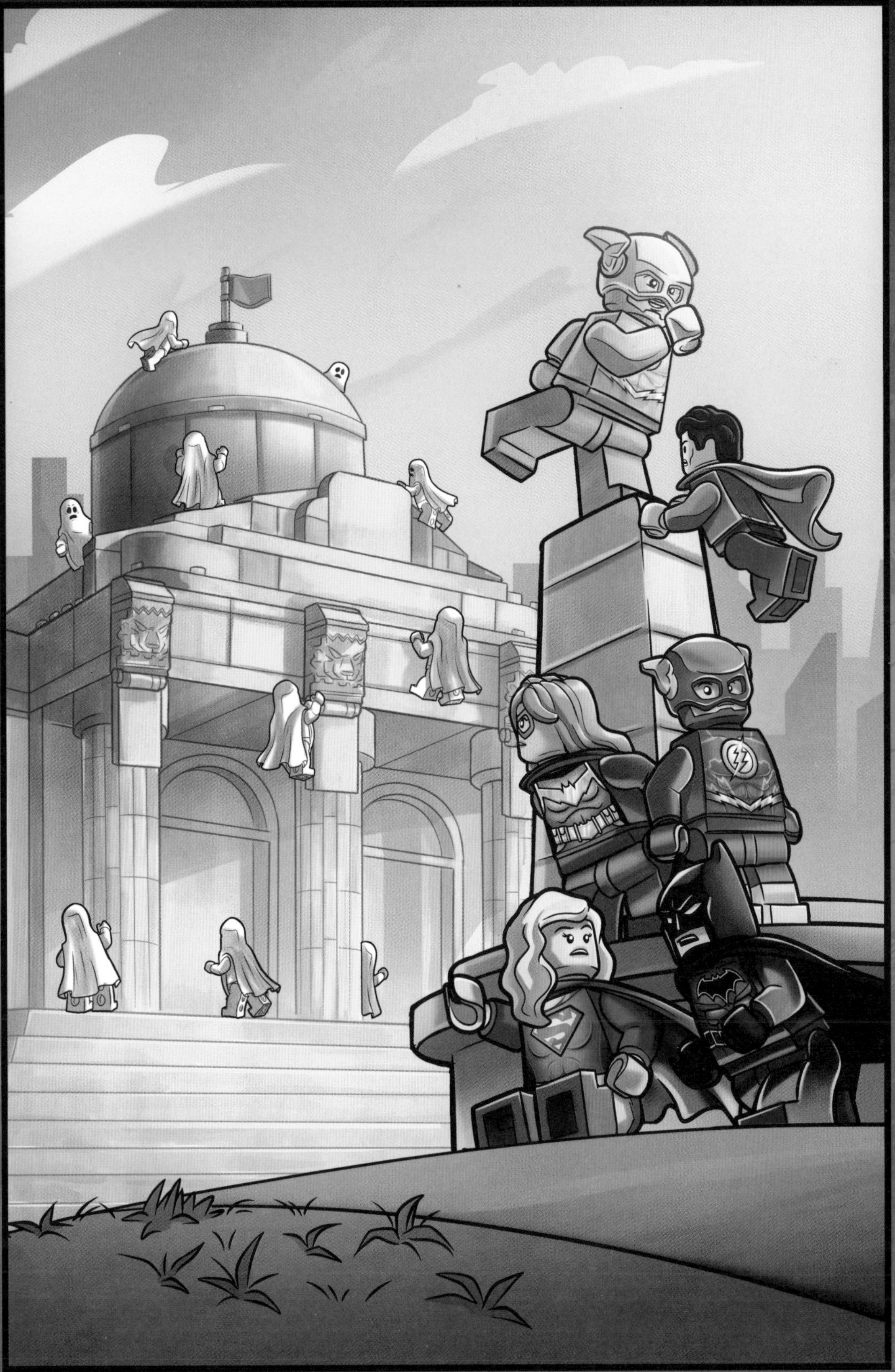

WHAM! A ghost lashed out with one of its arms and knocked into Supergirl.

Supergirl laughed. "Aw, you're so wobbly!"

The ghost stopped moving. It began to vibrate and glow with a creepy light. Then, to Supergirl's surprise, it hit her with a super-strong punch!

"Hey, I felt that!" she cried. The rest of the ghosts began to vibrate and glow.

"I'm coming!" called Superman. He flew toward the ghost that had punched Supergirl. *BANG!* He knocked it straight off the edge of the building. The Super Heroes watched as it fell. To their surprise, when it hit the ground, it sparked!

Superman and Supergirl flew down to get a better look. The ghost wasn't moving. Under the sheet, they saw a tangle of metal and wires.

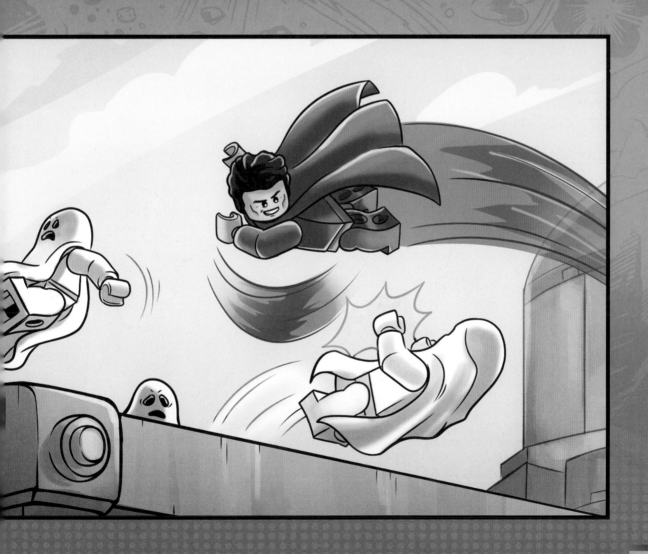

"Friends, I think these 'ghosts' are just robots," reported Superman. "But they look very high-tech. Who knows what they can do?"

"They can't fly. That's good," said Supergirl. "But they get stronger when they glow."

Batman tapped his chin thoughtfully. "If they're robots, then someone must be controlling them."

"Maybe we can figure out who!" said Batgirl. "I'll search for a signal."

Batgirl pulled a gadget with a long antenna out of her belt and switched it on. "Scanning . . . ," she said quietly. The device started beeping faster. Then, with a *PING*, all the lights on it turned green. "That's weird. Is the signal coming from . . . the museum basement?"

Batgirl spoke into her communicator. "Justice League," she said, "the bad guy is already inside the museum. These 'ghosts' are just a trick!"

"Then they're good at their job!" yelled The Flash. He was being grabbed by five glowing ghosts at once.

"Flash, get inside and find out what's going on," instructed Batman. "The rest of us can handle things out here."

"You got it, Batman." The Flash opened the museum door and ran through it. Some ghost robots inside tried to grab him again. But he was too fast for them.

He heard the sound of someone complaining up ahead. Then he heard an occasional *BANG*. He slowed down and poked his head around the corner quietly.

Bent over the Cosmic Treadmill, adjusting something with a wrench, was Reverse-Flash!

Reverse-Flash was one of The Flash's enemies. He was from the future, wore a yellow suit that looked like The Flash's suit, and had super-speed.

"*Arrrrgh!*" Reverse-Flash growled to himself. "Why won't it work? This technology is so hard to use! Of course, after I use this treadmill to travel to the past and stop the Justice League from ever being created, I won't have to worry! Heh-heh-heh."

"Reverse-Flash is here!" The Flash whispered into his communicator.

"Aha!" Batman responded. "That's why these robots are so advanced. Reverse-Flash must have made them from technology he brought with him from the future!"

"I have an idea," said Batgirl. "Flash, give us five minutes, and then lead Reverse-Flash out the front door."

The Flash raced across the room, straight past Reverse-Flash. He yanked the control panel off the Cosmic Treadmill.

"Can't time-travel without this, buddy!" The Flash teased, waving the control panel over his head. "Come and get it!" He raced up the stairs and into the main exhibit hall.

Reverse-Flash yelled and ran after him at top speed. On the main floor, he saw The Flash standing in the doorway to the Hall of Heroes. The Flash ran into the hall, with Reverse-Flash right behind him.

But once inside the hall, Reverse-Flash was forced to slow down and look around carefully. All around him were life-sized statues of Super Heroes fighting Super-Villains! The real Flash had to be somewhere in here . . . but where?

Reverse-Flash kept walking, looking all around him. "Wait a minute," muttered Reverse-Flash. "Why are there two Flashes here? There's only one statue of every other character!" He punched a Flash statue as hard as he could. *CRUNCH!* His fist smashed into hard stone.

"Ow!" he complained, shaking out his hand. He looked at the second Flash in the display, the one fighting The Cheetah.

The Flash blinked and grinned. "That sounds like my cue!" he said, laughing. He raced out of the exhibit.

"Get back here!" shouted Reverse-Flash. He chased The Flash through a door marked MIRROR MAZE. As he went inside, he saw that all around him were mirrors. They formed narrow hallways that led in every direction. "WHERE ARE YOU?" Reverse-Flash started breaking the mirrors, one by one.

The Flash rushed out of the maze.

Reverse-Flash followed, and the two began running circles around and around the museum.

"Whew," said The Flash. "This is making me dizzy!"

"Then stop," came Batgirl's voice over the communicator. "We're ready for you out here."

"Perfect!" The Flash ran out into the entrance hall. Reverse-Flash was right behind him as they charged outside.

Batman and the Super Heroes were waiting for them. They had built a cage right outside the front door. As The Flash threw the door open, Supergirl

swooped down and threw him into the air.

Reverse-Flash had no time to stop. He ran straight into the cage. Superman slammed the door shut behind him.

VMMMM! The cage powered up and glowed even brighter. Reverse-Flash tried to spin around quickly—but he only turned at normal speed. He looked down at himself in shock.

"That's right," Batgirl told him. "We built this cage from your tech. And we built it to take away your powers."

Batman nodded with satisfaction. "Looks like Central City is safe from all evildoers—"

"Including robot ghosts from the future!" finished The Flash.

JOKER CITY

Based on the story by **Philip Madden**

The Joker has a dastardly plan to transform Gotham City. He has a powerful and kooky new weapon—the Jokerizer ray! With it, he can turn anything silly! No one is safe from the criminal clown and his zany zapper. Can Batman and his friends keep the criminal clown from turning all of Gotham City into a Fun House? Or will The Joker have the last laugh?

It was just before the stroke of midnight as Batman patrolled the streets of Gotham City. Two scientists had been kidnapped this week. Suddenly, his butler appeared on the Batmobile's control panel.

"A report has just come in," Alfred said. "Another scientist is being kidnapped as we speak!"

"I'm on my way," said Batman. He took a closer look at the screen. "Alfred, I hope you're not trying on my costumes again."

"Of course not," sputtered Alfred.

"Then put away that costume you're not trying on," Batman replied as he took off.

Batman sped across town. He spotted The Joker's goons. They were tossing someone into the back of a truck.

The Joker spun around and pointed a strange device at the Batmobile and pressed a button. *WZZZZT!* The Batmobile transformed into a tiny ice cream truck.

Batman tried to get out, but he could barely move.

"Keep your cool!" The Joker cackled. "See what my new gadget can do? And it's only a prototype. Just wait until the real thing is ready. Gotham City will never be the same again!"

Batman watched the Super-Villain drive off.

It wasn't just Gotham City. Scientists were disappearing across the globe. It was time for Batman to call on the Justice League. Wonder Woman, Superman, The Flash, and Martian Manhunter assembled in the Batcave.

"I've determined that The Joker, Gorilla Grodd, and The Cheetah are behind the kidnappings," Batman explained. "And I'm afraid The Joker has his scientists working on something dangerous."

He filled in the group on his plan.

Meanwhile, across town, a scientist The Joker was trying to capture was fleeing for his life.

"He's getting away!" The Joker yelled to his thugs.

But when the scientist turned the corner, he ran right into Lobo, the intergalactic bounty hunter.

"Lose something?" Lobo asked The Joker.

"Lobo!" The Joker cried. "What are you doing here?"

"The word is you're up to no good," Lobo said. "And I want in on it."

Later, inside an abandoned balloon factory, Gorilla Grodd and The Cheetah were waiting.

"The scientists just finished the project!" Grodd exclaimed. "We can't wait to see what it is!"

The Joker laughed. "I guess we don't need this guy, then!"

Grodd spotted something sticking out of the scientist's pocket.

"A tracking device!" the huge ape bellowed.

The Joker shrugged. "Who cares! Just take a look at this!" He pressed a button. The floor opened, and a massive Joker head began to rise toward the roof.

"That's the secret project?" cried The Cheetah.

"Behold the Jokerizer!" cackled The Joker. "It's time to make this city a funnier place! Ready, aim, fire!"

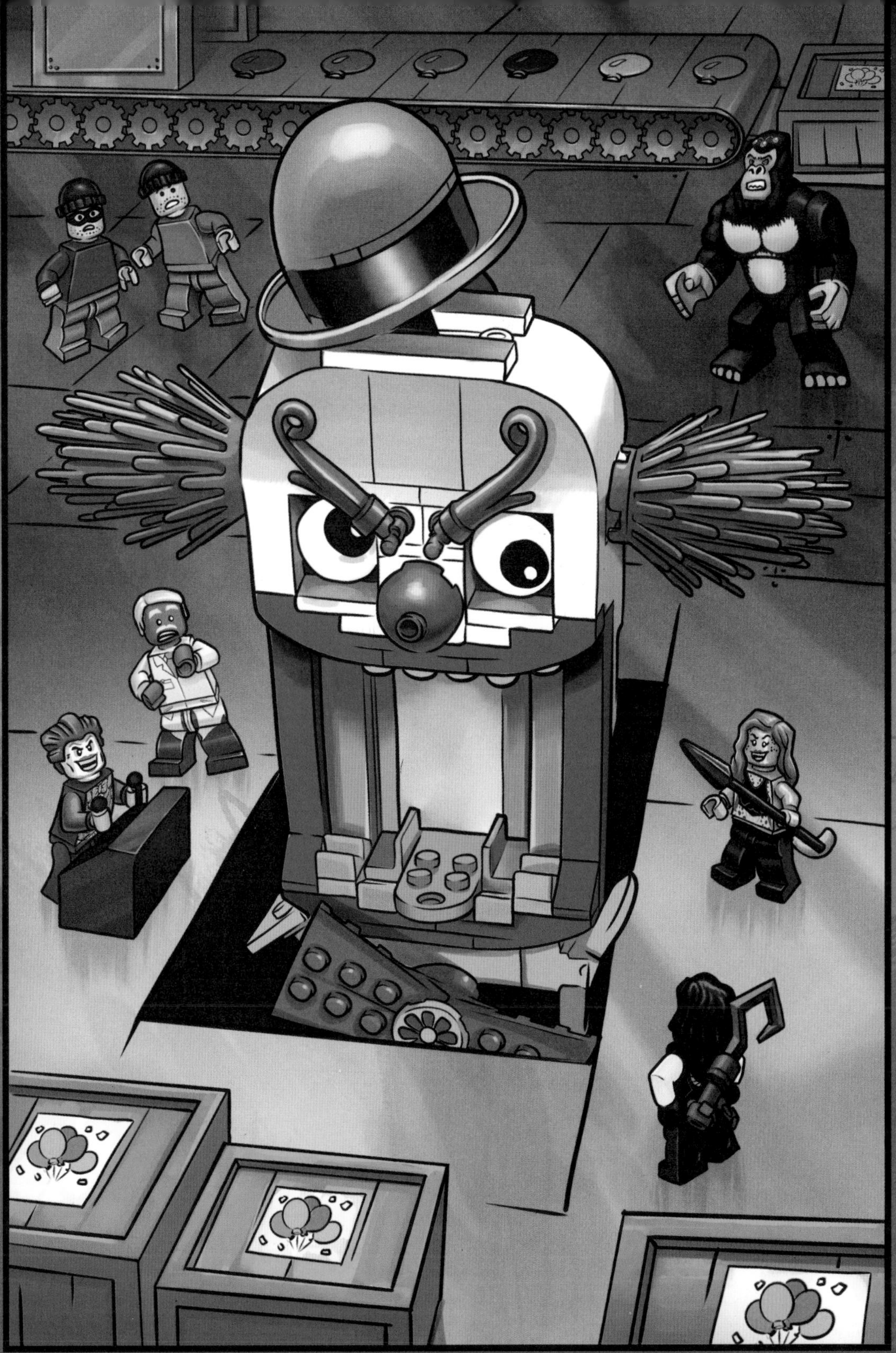

The Joker watched, entranced, as green lasers shot out of the Jokerizer's mouth. *BOOM!* Buildings were suddenly transformed into replicas of his grinning face. *ZIP!* Vehicles instantly converted into tiny clown cars. *CRASH!* Cars collided as the traffic lights changed to purple, blue, and orange. *ZING!* The citizens of Gotham City were turned into clowns!

Everyone stared in shock. A Jokerized city was terrifying to see.

"Stop right there!" a voice thundered.

The Joker spun around. "If it isn't Superman and his do-gooder friends," he said. "Well, you're too late. Today Gotham City, tomorrow the world!" He turned to the Super-Villains. "Show these Justice Losers what we think of uninvited guests!"

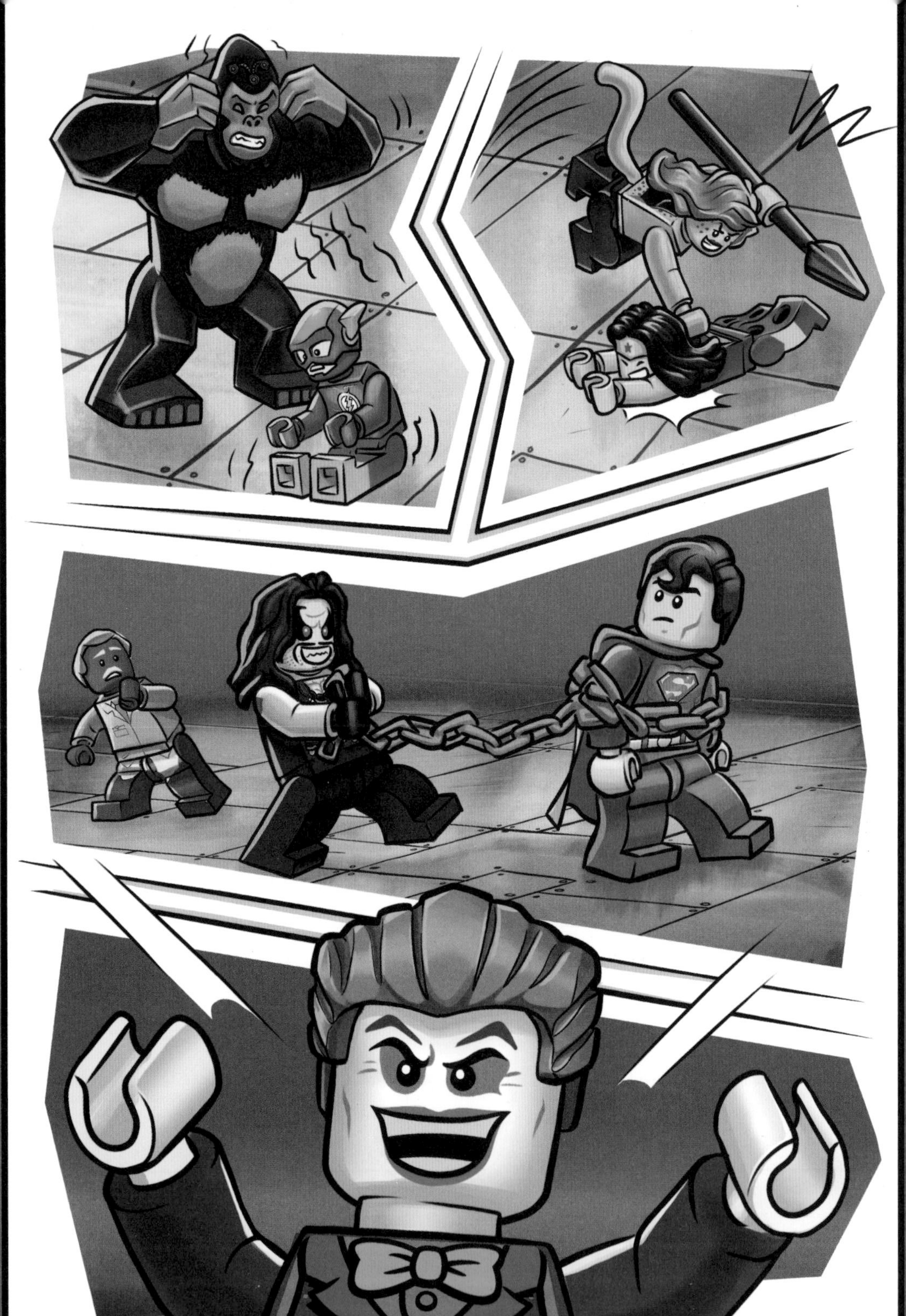

Lobo grabbed Superman and wrapped him in chains. The Cheetah pounced on Wonder Woman, taking her down. And Grodd used his mind control to force The Flash to his knees.

"That was as easy as taking candy from a baby, and just as fun, too!" The Joker exclaimed. He raised his arms. "Welcome to Joker City, where everyone's just like me!"

Grodd scowled. "Just like you? Why can't it be Grodd City instead?"

The Cheetah nodded. "Cheetah City sounds better to me!"

The Joker snarled. "This is my beautiful city!"

"You're wrong, Joker," Lobo said. "Everything in your city is boring!"

"Not cool, Lobo!" The Joker spluttered. "I thought you were on my side!"

"Nope, never was," Martian Manhunter said as he transformed. "Surprise! I'm not Lobo."

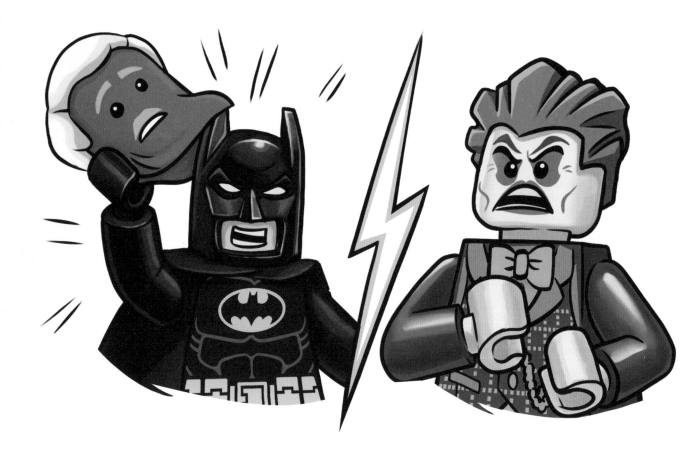

Just then, the scientist stepped forward and removed the rubber mask he'd been wearing, revealing another mask underneath.

"Batman!" cried The Joker. He pulled out the smaller prototype of the Jokerizer and pointed it at him. But Batman tossed a Batarang and knocked the gadget out of his hand.

The Flash grabbed the gadget and handed it to Batman. Then he took off his cap to reveal a special headband. "This deflected your mind control, Grodd!" he said.

While the Super-Villains stared in shock, Wonder Woman caught them in her magic lasso.

Batman glanced at the prototype. "As I suspected," he said. "Those genius scientists added a reverse switch!" He pointed the prototype at the Jokerizer and pressed the button. In the blink of an eye, The Joker's pride and joy disintegrated into a pile of bricks.

Superman and Martian Manhunter quickly assembled the bricks. They made a giant tube and pointed it at the city.

Batman aimed the prototype into the tube, which made its power one hundred times stronger. In an instant, everything returned to normal.

Everyone cheered. Batman had returned the city to normal . . . except for one building. The Cheetah and Grodd groaned as a prison shaped like The Joker came into view.

The Cheetah scowled. "Captured in Joker Jail?"

Grodd growled at The Joker. "I'll get you for this."

"Say, guys," The Joker said to the Justice League, "can you make sure I get a cell far away from those two? They don't have a sense of humor!"

CYBORG'S BIG RESCUE!

Based on the story by **Philip Madden**

The Justice League is in a world of trouble! An evil alien robot wants to take over the planet. Even with their combined powers, this enemy may be too powerful! Maybe Cyborg can help— but he just won't pay attention! Will Batman and the other Super Heroes be able to foil the alien's out-of-this world plan? And, more important, will Cyborg actually listen to his friends?

"Stop, thief!" cried Superman.

Batman was about to throw a Batarang at the fleeing suspect. But Wonder Woman stopped him.

"False alarm," she said. "He was just jogging."

Superman shrugged. "Sorry," he said. "When I invited you to visit Metropolis, I was thinking there would be a little more action."

"Look on the bright side," said Batman. "It's not like Watchtower. Can you imagine how boring it is up there for Cyborg?"

Just then, Batman's wrist communicator beeped.

"Look, here he is now!" Batman exclaimed.

Cyborg appeared on the screen. "There was a break-in at Metropolis City Museum," he said excitedly.

"Catwoman and The Cheetah were caught on camera stealing a bunch of crystal cats. They took them to an abandoned mansion at the edge of the city."

"Now things are finally getting interesting!" said Batman. "Cyborg, can you give us—"

"Some ideas?" said Cyborg. "Yes! I think you should take the Batwing, swoop in, and show them who's boss!"

"No, he means—" Wonder Woman started to say.

"Or you could fly your invisible plane and launch a surprise attack!" Cyborg suggested.

Superman sighed. "No, that's not what—"

"Didn't mean to leave you out, Superman," said Cyborg. "You could . . . zoom in and knock them out with a powerful punch!"

"Can you just give us the coordinates, Cyborg?" Superman asked.

Cyborg sighed as he keyed in the location.

The crumbling mansion was surrounded by a thicket of gnarled old trees. It glowed eerily in the moonlight.

They crept up to the building and peered through a shattered stained glass window.

Inside the ruined mansion, twelve crystal cats sat in a circle. Each was emitting an unearthly green light. Catwoman and The Cheetah stood in the middle, looking like zombies. A hooded figure turned to them.

"Thousands of years ago, while visiting Earth, I found twelve powerful crystals," the figure said. "I hid them in a cave. But when I returned, they were gone. I discovered that an ancient tribe took them, turning them into cat statues. Luckily, I remembered you two talented cat burglars could fetch them for me! And now that I have activated the crystals, Earth will be mine!"

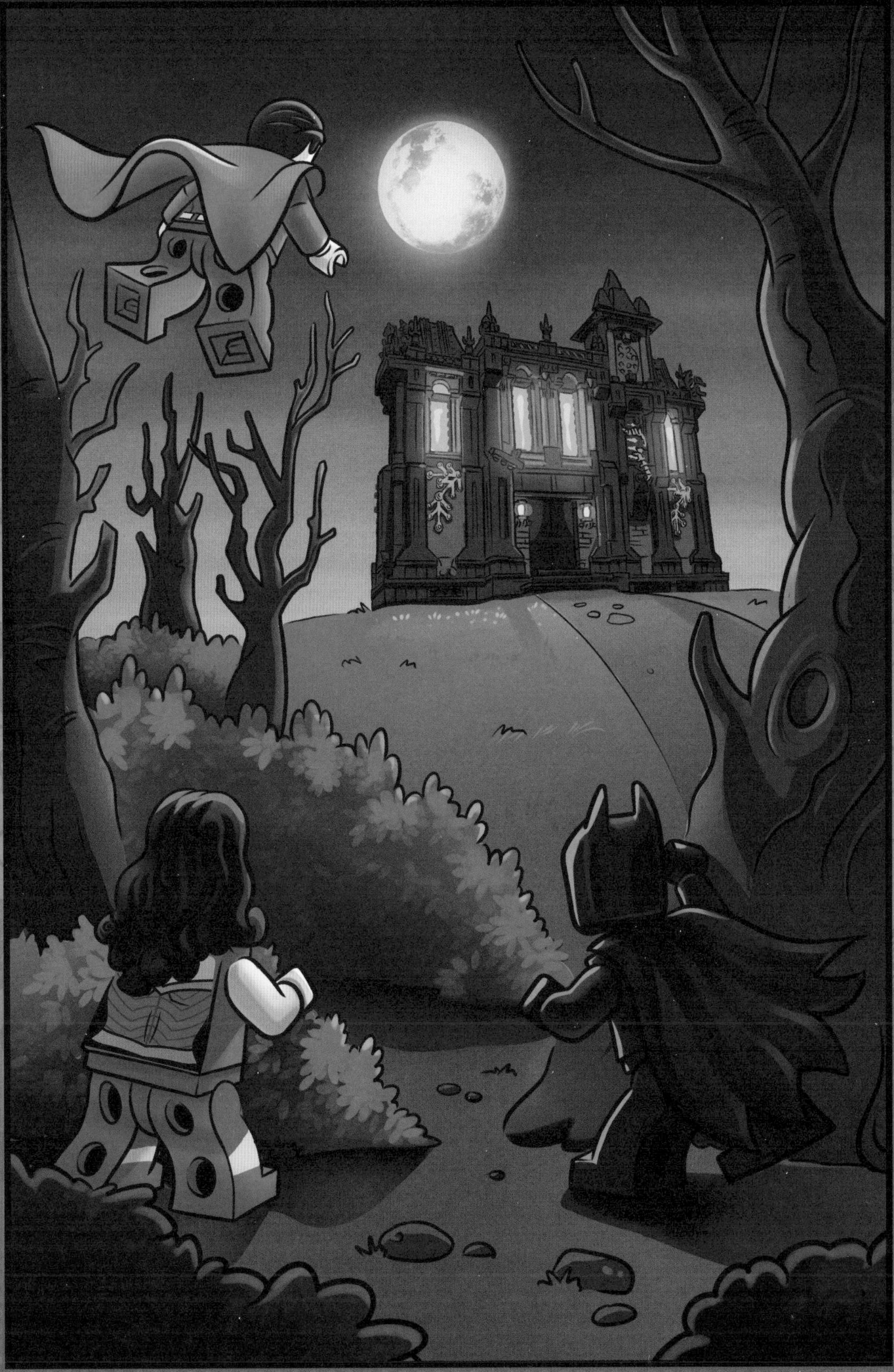

"Why do Super-Villains always explain themselves in long speeches?" asked Wonder Woman.

"Let's find out who it is first," said Batman.

Superman took a deep breath and blew the hood right off the villain's head.

"Brainiac!" Superman exclaimed. The extraterrestrial robot was one of his greatest foes.

Brainiac spun around. "Look who's here to stop me! But you're too late, Justice League! Welcome my grand army!"

The crystals glowed brightly, creating a circle of pure white light. They had opened a portal! Dozens of robots began streaming through from Brainiac's world!

"My clones will overwhelm this planet. Soon it will be mine!" Brainiac cried.

"Not on my watch!" shouted Superman. He and Wonder Woman flew into the air and began fighting the clones.

But with every clone they destroyed, a dozen more appeared.

"There are too many!" cried Wonder Woman. "Cyborg!" she said into her communicator. "We need your help!"

Cyborg teleported there in a flash.

"Cyborg!" said Superman. "We need you to—"

"Beat up these clones! Got it!" cried Cyborg. "Punch faster? No problemo!"

Superman was losing his patience. "Cyborg, you need to listen!" he shouted. "Brainiac is a cyborg, too. Only you can shut him down!"

Cyborg turned and opened his mouth, but to Superman's horror, Brainiac's voice came out instead.

"Cyborg can't hear you," he snarled. "I'm in control now!"

Wave after wave of robot clones poured out of the portal. Wonder Woman paused to look at the cat crystals. Were they attached to a machine that was giving them power?

"If I could just destroy that machine, it might close the portal," she said. She stared at Catwoman and The Cheetah, standing motionless. Could they help? She flicked her Lasso of Truth, ensnaring the two.

The lasso returned them to normal and Wonder

Woman let them know what Brainiac had done
to them.

"He used us!" Catwoman hissed.

"He will regret it soon," The Cheetah snorted.

"But how is he powering the crystals?"
Catwoman asked.

"With that," said Wonder Woman, pointing to
the machine.

"Let's destroy it!" The Cheetah said.

The two felines pounced, tearing Brainiac's machine to pieces. Instantly, the portal closed, and the remaining clones crashed to the ground.

Brainiac spun around to see what was happening. In that moment, he lost his mental hold on Cyborg. "Nooooo!" he cried.

Cyborg was back in full control of his mind and body. Cyborg focused on the robot with every atom of his being. By listening closely, he figured out Brainiac's programming.

Cyborg grinned. "Powering down," he said.

Suddenly, Brainiac's eyes bulged. He collapsed to the ground, motionless.

"The Earth is safe," said Superman.

Batman began gathering the crystal cats. "It looks like two are missing," he said.

Superman looked around. "And so are Catwoman and The Cheetah!"

"Let them go," said Wonder Woman. "Without the missing crystals, Brainiac will never be able to open the portal again."

Batman nodded. "It's time to put Brainiac where he belongs," he said. He turned to Cyborg. "The honor is yours."

When Brainiac finally woke up, he found himself in a cell.

"Darn you, Justice League!" he cried. "I'm going to get even if it's the last thing I do!"

Turning to Cyborg with a smile, Batman said, "Good thing this robot has an off switch."

THE FLASH'S CHALLENGE!

Based on the story by **Philip Madden**

Some very coldhearted Super-Villains give The Flash an impossible challenge. There's too much to do and not enough time—even for the famous speedster! Batman and the other Super Heroes are worried—but The Flash doesn't want any help. Is there any way he'll be able to do it all on his own? Can he beat the odds and beat the clock to defeat this team of bad guys?

"Calling the Justice League's annual budget meeting to order," Superman announced. He looked around the room. "Hey, has anyone seen The Flash?"

Just then, the door flew open. There was a blur of red and yellow as The Flash raced inside and slid into his seat.

"Sorry I'm late," he said. "It has been a really busy day. I rescued a sinking ship, foiled a bank robbery,

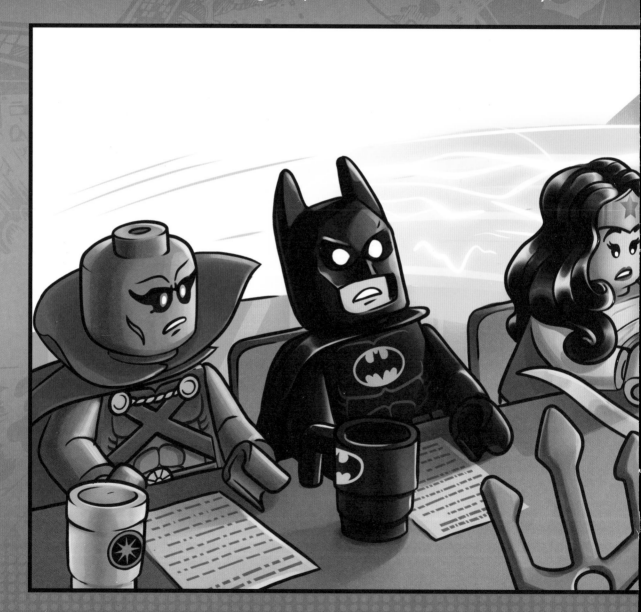

and stopped a runaway train. Then, on my way here, I saved a cat stuck in a tree."

Batman leaned forward. "You know, Flash, you can always ask us for help."

The Flash shook his head. "Thanks for the offer," he said. "But I'm The Flash, the fastest person on the planet. I can do it myself."

Then something on the TV got their attention.

Everyone stared as the faces of Captain Cold, Frost, and Mr. Freeze filled the screen. They were three of the Justice League's greatest—and coldest—enemies.

"Greetings from the Frozen Trinity!" said Mr. Freeze. "We have a special announcement for The Flash."

"You see this hunk of tin?" asked Captain Cold. "Well, it's all yours if you can complete our challenge!"

"That's Jay Garrick's!" The Flash exclaimed. "They must have stolen it from The Flash Museum!" Jay was the very first Flash. His helmet was the most precious artifact in the entire museum.

"You will be given eight tasks. If you complete them all, the helmet is yours," said Frost.

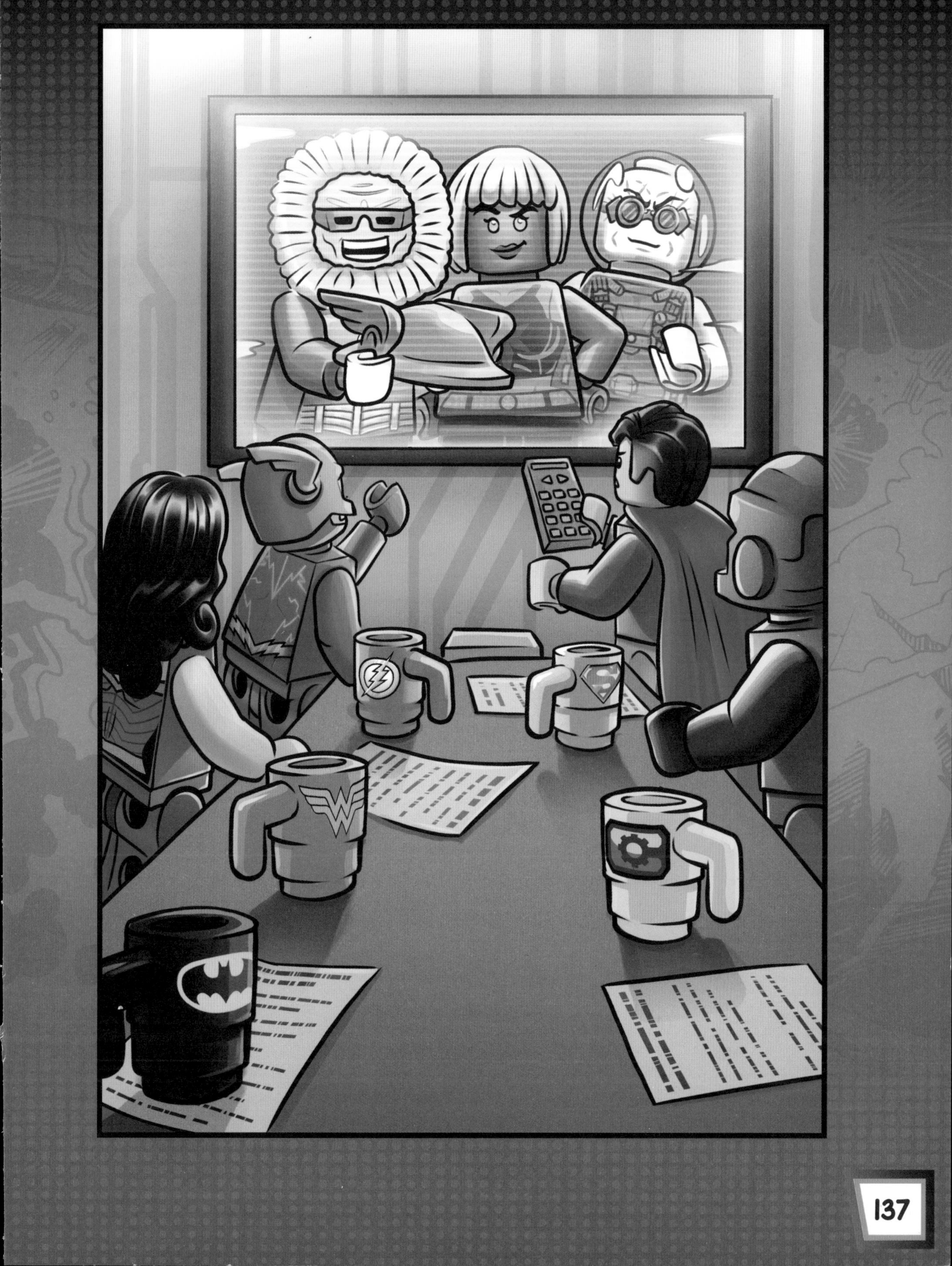

The Flash was livid. "I've got to get that helmet back!" he said.

"We're ready to help any way we can!" said Aquaman. "This may need teamwork."

The Flash stood up. "Thanks, but no thanks," he said. He stood and sped out of the room.

When The Flash arrived, a crowd of excited onlookers was waiting.

A huge screen flickered to life. An image of the Frozen Trinity appeared for a moment, then was replaced by a list.

EIGHT TASKS FOR THE FLASH

1) Knock out Solomon Grundy with one punch.
2) Remove Lex Luthor's armor and put a red wig on his head.
3) Lock Poison Ivy in a cage.
4) Swipe Sinestro's power ring.
5) Catch Reverse-Flash.
6) Defeat Killer Croc in a wrestling match.
7) Stuff The Joker into Commissioner Gordon's locker.
8) Bring them all to jail!

"One more thing," said Frost. "You have to do it all in ONE MINUTE!"

The Flash said, "Start the countdown. And try not to blink, or you'll miss everything!"

In a secret lair with ice-covered walls, Frost, Captain Cold, and Mr. Freeze cackled and watched the action.

"It doesn't even matter how many tasks he completes," Mr. Freeze said. "With all the other Super-Villains in jail, we'll be the only game in town. Then we can bring about what we've always wanted—Eternal Winter. Nothing but cold and darkness forever!"

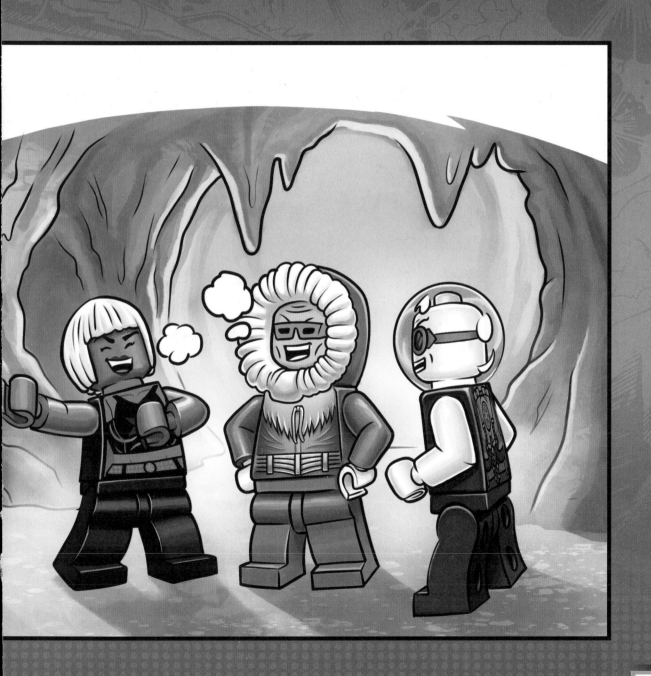

"Though I really wouldn't mind seeing Luthor in a bright-red clown wig," added Frost.

"Well, there he is, red wig and all," said Captain Cold, pointing to one of the screens.

Frost turned around and gasped. The countdown had barely started, and on the screen, she saw that every villain had already been taken out!

"Impossible!" shouted Captain Cold. "Time for Eternal Winter!"

Suddenly, the door burst open, and in came The Flash.

"Eternal Winter?" he said. "How about Eternal Incarceration?" He glanced up at the clock.

"Looks like it's time for me to take you to jail."

"You and what army?" said Mr. Freeze.

The Flash smiled. And at that very moment, a second Flash came in wearing Luthor's armor!

The Frozen Trinity stared in disbelief as a third Flash walked in. Flashes four, five, and six arrived next.

"What's going on?" demanded Mr. Freeze.

"Simple," said Flash number one. "I figured out why you wanted me to capture the other Super-Villains. So I got a little help from my friends."

"That's right," said a Flash as he transformed back into Martian Manhunter. The others removed their masks. It was Batman, Wonder Woman, Cyborg, and Aquaman!

"And now," said The Flash, "you owe me a helmet."

"Not so fast, Flash," said Mr. Freeze.

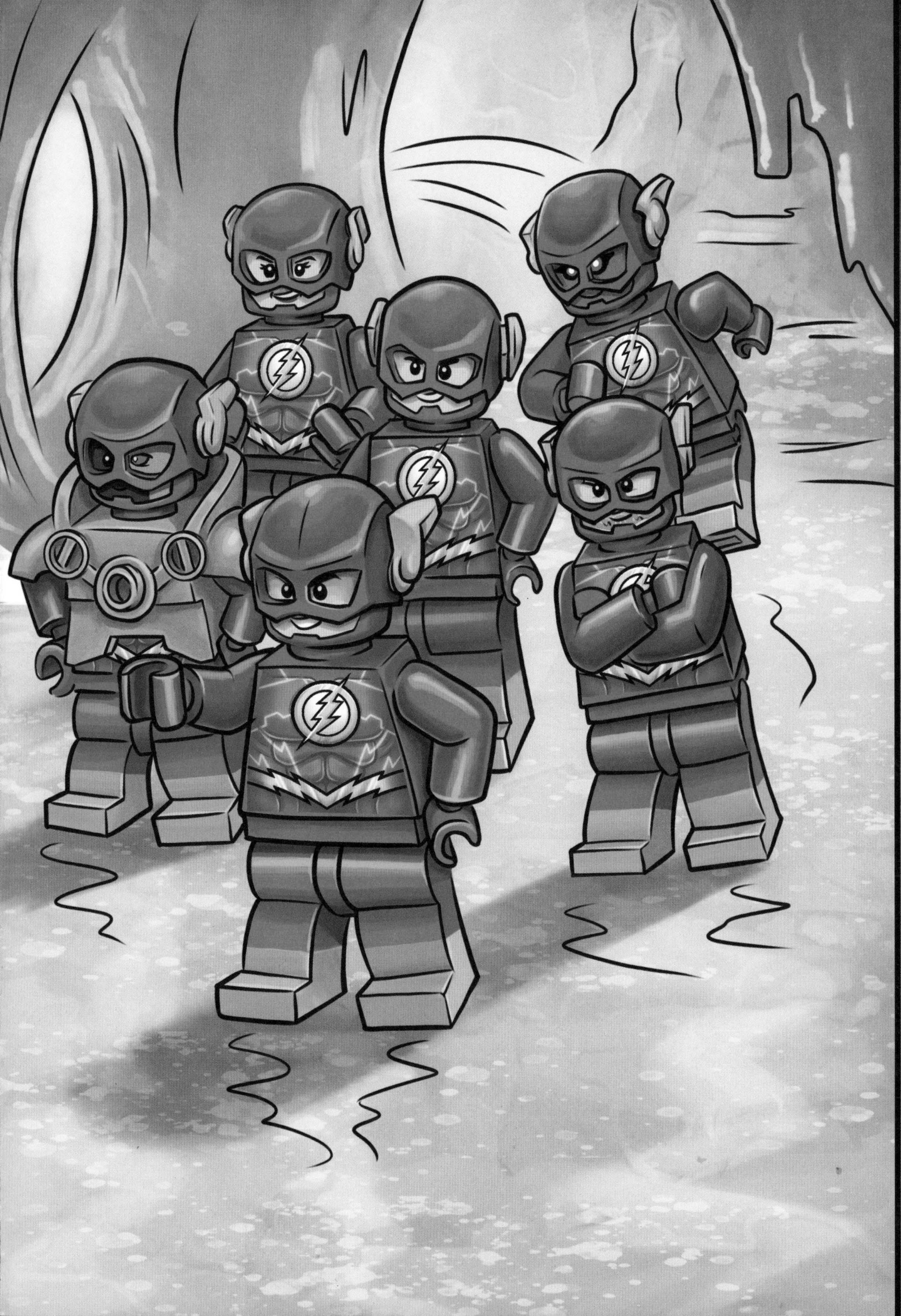

BOOM! Just then, the seventh Flash burst through the wall. He grabbed Captain Cold and Mr. Freeze.

The final Flash removed his mask. It was Superman. "I see you forgot how to count," he said to the Super-Villains.

The Flash zoomed back to the main square, where the crowd was waiting.

He held the winged helmet aloft for the world to see. "The Frozen Trinity is on their way to jail! And Jay Garrick's helmet will soon be back where it belongs," he said. Everyone cheered.

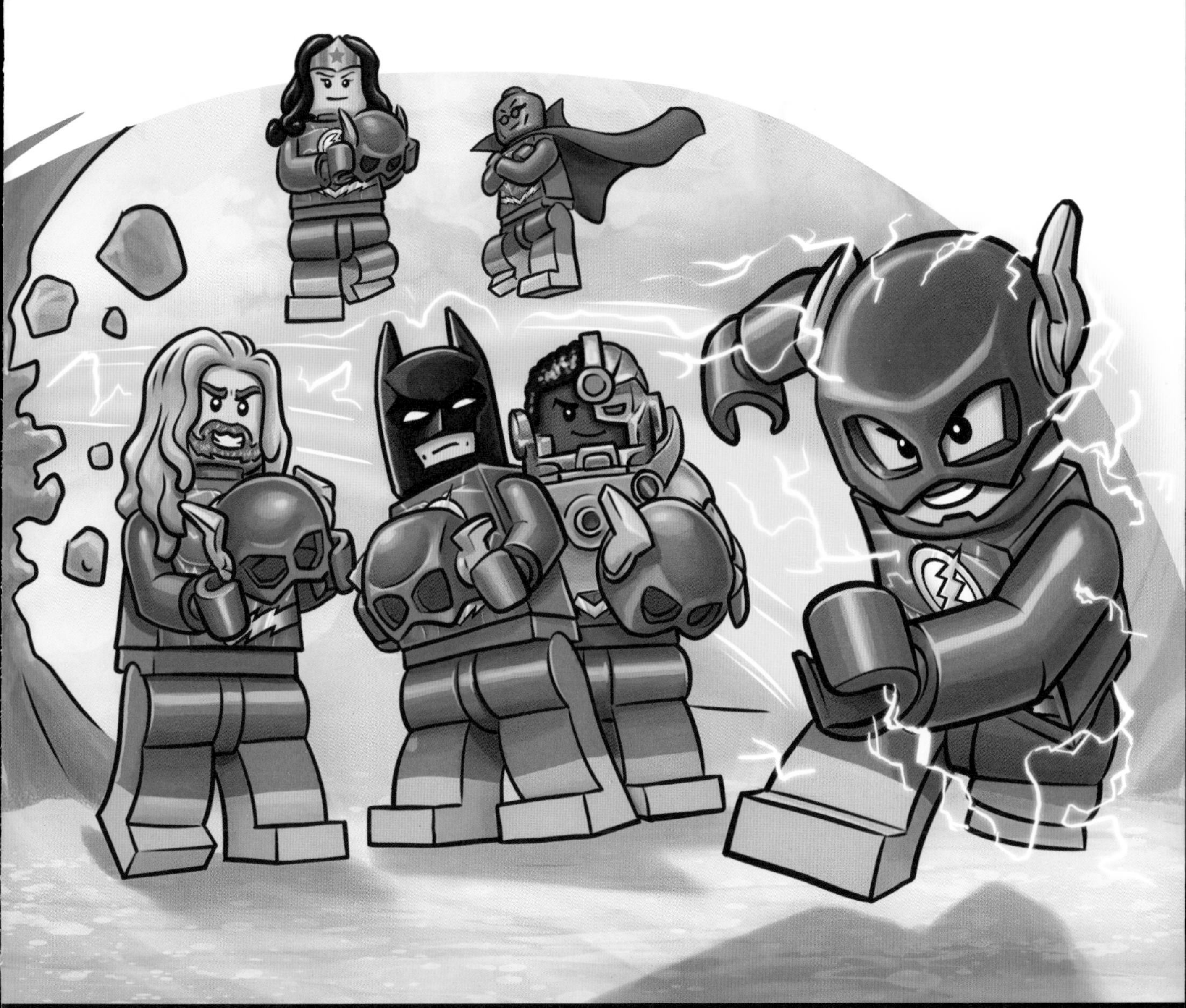

Meanwhile, over in the exercise yard at Arkham Asylum, the Frozen Trinity was backed into a corner.

"The way I see it," said The Joker, "you guys owe us, big-time."

"That's right," said Lex Luthor. "And you can start by building us an outdoor ice rink."

"Talk about Eternal Winter!" Frost said. "This one is never going to end!"

GLOSSARY

Aquaman
He is the King of Atlantis and a hero who protects the world above and below the oceans.

Batgirl
She's a crime-fighting computer genius who fights side by side with Batman.

Batman
He is a self-made Super Hero who keeps the streets of Gotham City safe. By day, he is the billionaire known as Bruce Wayne.

Captain Cold
One of The Flash's oldest enemies, he'll steal anything that's not nailed down. His heart is not entirely cold—sometimes he helps the good guys.

Catwoman
An expert burglar and jewel thief who enjoys sparring with Batman.

Croc
This brawny Super-Villain lives in the sewers below Gotham City, emerging only to wreak havoc and commit crimes.

Cyborg
A teen Super Hero who is part man, part machine. He has the ability to interface with computer systems.

Frost
This cold crook loves to freeze her opponents. She can project ice and snow from her fingertips.

Gorilla Grodd
A hyper-intelligent ape who can read people's minds. He is a great enemy of The Flash.

Harley Quinn
She works with The Joker to cause trouble for Batman—and she loves a good laugh.

Lex Luthor

This brilliant billionaire is considered by the Justice League to be the most dangerous man alive. He is Superman's greatest foe and has a warsuit that gives him great strength, special weapons, and the ability to fly.

Martian Manhunter

This alien has many superpowers, including the ability to shape-shift.

Mr. Freeze

This cryogenics (the science studying the effects of cold) expert wears a special suit so he can survive in above-freezing temperatures.

Reverse-Flash

This Super-Villain is from the future and travels through time to attack The Flash.

Superman and Supergirl

These two aliens from Krypton use their superpowers to protect Earth.

The Cheetah

Part human, part cheetah, this Super-Villain is the sworn enemy of Wonder Woman.

The Flash

He is the Fastest Man Alive. Over the years, there have been three Flashes, one after the other.

The Joker

As the fearsome Clown Prince of Crime, he is Batman's archnemesis.

The Penguin

Oswald Cobblepot is a criminal mastermind who uses weaponized umbrellas.

Wonder Woman

An Amazon warrior princess, she is a beacon of hope and peace.

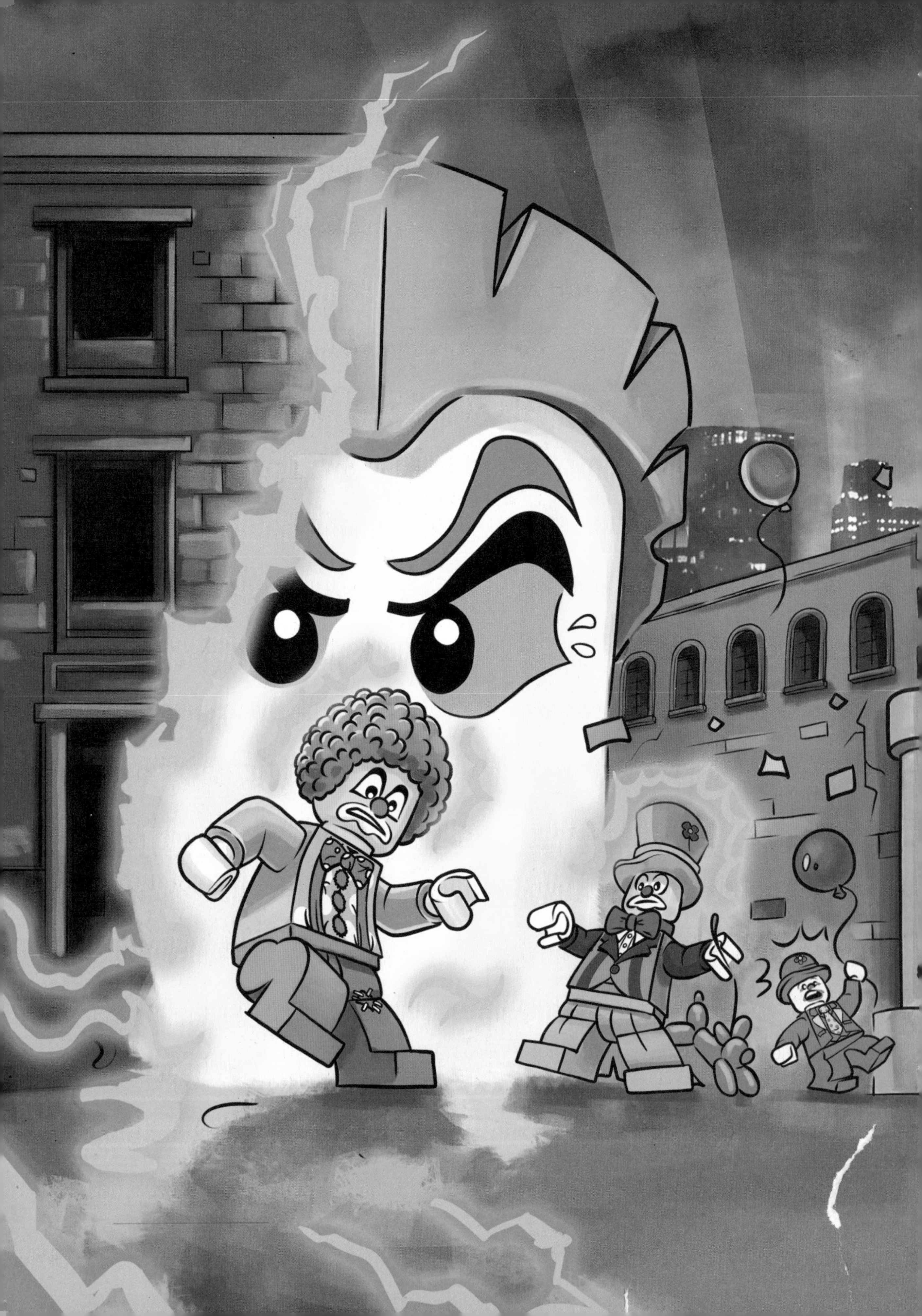